ESCAPE TO THE HIGHLANDS
Published by Keira Montclair
Copyright © 2022 by Keira Montclair

Printed in the USA.

Cover Design and Interior Format

ESCAPE TO THE HIGHLANDS

KEIRA MONTCLAIR

CHAPTER ONE

The Lowlands of Scotland, early summer of 1255

SYMON MACKINNON'S LIFE was over.
    Not because of the Lowland Chieftain standing in front of him with his sword drawn or the three others next to him reflecting the same posture. Or even the chains that bound his own hands behind the post he was seated against.

Nor was his life over due to the other forty guards carrying various weaponry—clubs, lit torches, swords, bows, axes. None of those frightened him.

Not even the pain shooting out of the ragged wound ripped into his leg by some sword.

It was what was missing.

This was the Lowlands of Scotland, MacKinnon land, presently occupied by a horde of villainous Lowlanders. His father's castle, where Symon was raised with his siblings, the very place his sire had married his mother, Cynthia. Ronan and Cynthia had brought four children into the world who had lived. Symon was the eldest and had two younger brothers, Craeg and Boyd. Alicia, his only sister, was the wee bairn of the family. But he didn't see evidence of any of them, dead or alive, in the courtyard in front of him.

MacKinnon Castle was no more. His father lay dead not far away, his mother's bloody shawl evidence that she was not far from his sire. He was certain the small mound behind his father was his mother, but he couldn't bring himself to look at her. The rest of his family were nowhere to be seen. Symon did not know how long he had been unconscious and as he roused now, he felt haunted by the missing time. What had happened to his family, to his clan, while he was knocked out? All he could tell for sure was that the courtyard was covered with blood and bodies. MacKinnon blood and MacKinnon bodies.

There wasn't a red plaid in sight, except on dead bodies. The thatched roofs of his clansmen's huts still burned inside the curtain wall, which was pocked with gaping holes from where stones had been wrenched out of place. He could even see the crops through the open gate, nothing but smoldering ashes in the many fields on their land. Men continued to carry furniture out of the keep into the courtyard, only to empty the contents and line the various chests and chairs in the courtyard for all to see.

Ransacked first, then to be burned to ashes.

And bodies? Bodies were everywhere.

"Kill me and be done with it," he whispered. Memories of what had happened before he'd been knocked out returned to him, but how he wished they hadn't. He wished he had no memory of what had happened at all. He wished he had died with his sire.

He had no reason to live.

The man in front of him had plunged his bloody sword into Ronan MacKinnon's chest. His father's hand had clutched the weapon as if to stop it, but the polished steal had moved through Ronan's grip and entered his heart and Symon had seen the blood spilling from between his father's fingers, still wrapped around the blade. All these years, he'd considered his father to be indestructible because the man trained so hard and for so many years. Tall, broad-shouldered, and muscular, seeing him fall was one of the worst memories Symon would ever have.

His father's body limp on the cold stone, blood everywhere.

Pouring blood until it could only seep because there was no more left to bleed, his dear father's body crumpling to the ground in front of him. Death in an instant to the strong, beloved chieftain of Clan MacKinnon. That much Symon had been witness to. He'd begged to be next, wished to be next, to be killed so quickly, with the same pain as his sire had suffered.

And all their people.

But the men had surrounded him and beat him until he'd passed out, every fist leaving a memory and the subsequent pain he wished would leave him.

"'Tis about time ye awakened." The chieftain of Clan Chisolm smiled at him, an evil grin that Symon would love to punch until he knocked every one of his teeth out. Instinctively, he tugged at the chains that bound his hands until he felt the warm sensation of fresh blood running down his left wrist.

"Just kill me. Be done with it. Why do ye wait? It surely is not due to any slight amount of compassion you have within ye, Chisolm. We all know ye have naught."

His voice came out in a roar that surprised him more than anyone else. "Why?" The bastard came over and grabbed Symon's long dark hair, wrenching his head back until it struck the wooden post he was bound to, but he did not flinch. Would not give his captor the satisfaction. "I'll tell ye why. We wish for yer treasures. The famous MacKinnon treasures you've collected over the years."

"I know naught of what ye speak. We have nae treasures. A few gold coins ye are welcome to take on yer way out. But 'tis naught else here for ye."

Chisolm's head fell back and laughed, releasing Symon, then looking at the three men next to him, his companions joining in his laughter.

"He thinks we'll believe him, Chief," the tallest man said. "We know of the treasures."

"He's a fool, is he not, Malcolm?"

"He is," the man said, nodding his agreement. "A fool."

Chisolm turned back to Symon. "Think ye we know naught of the whisky yer grandfather distilled into the golden liquid as fine as any king has ever had? Rumor has it there are casks and barrels of the fine liquid hidden in caves and in your cellars. But we found none."

Symon spit at the man's feet. "And ye'll never find it. We have little left. What my sire distilled was thrown out. He forgot the recipe, tried to improve upon it, failed, and then couldn't recall the old. 'Tis lost with the caskets of the buried."

Chisolm knelt down in front of him. "I'm going to allow ye to live another day. Let ye spend a night in the dungeon of yer own castle, but only one night. I wish to inspect everything that comes out of that keep before I burn it. If I'm lucky, I'll find yer gold coins, but either way, ye'll tell me all on the morrow."

Chisolm nodded to one of his guards, the largest one in the group standing behind him. The man stepped forward, swung his fist back, and brought it forward, connecting with Symon's face.

He plunged into a welcomed world of darkness.

———◆◆◆———

When he awakened the next day, he forced himself to a sitting position, not surprised to find himself in the dark, odiferous dungeon, but surprised to see he was not alone. "Are ye no' one of the MacKinnon stable lads?"

"Aye," the flame-haired lad replied, sitting across from him in the same cell.

Symon scratched his head, wondering how many critters he now had living inside his dark hair. He recognized the lad as a hard-working boy, but he couldn't recall his name. "Yer name?"

"Finn of the MacKinnons. My sire was Finnian.

Said someday when I earned it, he'd call me Finnian too."

He caught the word he hated most to hear, though it never bothered him before his clan was reduced to rubble. "Was? Yer sire is gone as mine is?"

The lad nodded, his red locks bouncing about his face. "Aye, my sire died two years ago. But our chieftain is dead for certain? The Chisolms killed him when they attacked?"

"They killed him in front of me. Said 'twas the only reason they'd allow me to live—to torture me into telling them where our treasures are."

"Have they tortured ye yet?"

"Nay. How did ye survive? Seemed everyone was dead when I was in the courtyard."

"I hid. They found me, but neither Fagan nor Malcolm were around so they said I had to stay down here with ye. They'd wait and torture me with ye, he said."

He hated to ask the question but he had to know. "Did they beat ye, Finn?"

Bairns were the one weakness in his otherwise impenetrable constitution. He hated to see men abuse anyone smaller than they were: lads, lasses, women.

He hated the bullies in the world.

"Nay. They threw me in here and said they would deal with me when they dealt with ye." He hung his head just as a loaf of bread was tossed in through the window.

Symon caught it and took a bite but then

looked at the scrawny child in front of him. "Here, ye may have the rest."

"Nay, ye are the nobleman, no' me. Ye deserve it."

"Lad, am I no' heir to the chieftain here?"

"Aye."

"And do ye believe me when I say my sire is dead?"

"Aye. I didnae see him die, but I saw him on the ground. Yer mother and both of yer brothers were struck down too."

"Then that makes me the laird of Clan MacKinnon. No matter the size, I'm ordering ye to eat the bread. I had a bite, the rest is yers to eat."

He gingerly reached for the bread, an expression of sheer surprise crossing his face when he had it in his hand. "Ye didnae take it back," he said with a grin. "Many thanks to ye, but I'll save ye a hunk."

The lad devoured half the loaf while Symon just watched. He grabbed a sip of water from the bucket that had been left in the cell, then set it down, observing the lad even more. Why had he made that odd comment?

"Ye thought I would take it back?"

The lad's eyes jumped from one side of the cell to the other before he spoke, as if faeries were to jump in through the walls if he answered poorly. "Forgive me, Chief, but ye often did it to other men when ye were...rather..." He cleared his throat.

"Finish yer statement, lad. I'm clearly no' in a position to hurt ye. I think we may be the only MacKinnons left." He pushed himself up to a sitting position where he could lean against the cold stone wall. The condition of the cell he was in was beyond reprehensible. Glad they hadn't made frequent use of the dungeon when his sire was alive, the least they could have done was clean up the dirt and the rodent droppings. His view of his previous life and his love of the sweet amber liquid was changing quickly.

"Ye would do it when ye were deep in yer cups." Finn dropped his gaze after he finished his sentence. "Offer someone the breath of life, then take it back."

"Ye shouldnae be embarrassed, Finn MacKinnon. I should be, no' ye."

The lad ate in silence, giving Symon the chance to reflect on his situation in life, both past and present. He'd been too deep in his cups too often. He liked his ale, even more liked to keep his own supply of the golden breath of life his grandsire had made with his own still. His father had been after him many a time to learn the brewing techniques because the MacKinnon golden liquid was the best in all the land, but he'd been too busy.

Too busy drinking it, enjoying the whisky made with special barley heated until it was pure gold. The breath of life indeed.

Oh, he'd gone along once or twice and followed his grandsire as he explained the process, and if he were to tell the truth, he'd been certain to lock all his grandsire's secrets in his mind, but it would do him little good in his present situation.

He could definitely use a goblet of liquid gold at present.

The clang of the key in the door caught his attention before the footsteps caught him. Malcolm Chisholm, eldest of the sons of the chieftain, rattled the door as he opened it. He stood with a twisted grin on his face and stared at Symon. "Will ye come willingly or shall I have ye brought in chains?"

"I'll come willingly. I doubt I can fight off three score men with only two fists. Especially if ye vow to leave the boy alone. Ye have no reason to punish a lad of only ten summers."

"One and ten," Finn mumbled under his breath.

"I'll leave him here for now. We want ye first."

Symon nodded and pushed himself to his feet, forcing him to acknowledge all the pain and aching spots in his body thanks to his captors. Each bruise had a part in building the fury he would need to fight.

If given the chance.

He used his practiced skills of observation as he marched ahead of Malcolm, down the passageway where he saw no other prisoners, up the staircase, and out into the gray skies of early summer. He blinked against the brightness of the overcast day, his eyes slowly adjusting after his time in the dungeon cell. Refusing to react to the spitting aimed at him by the guards he passed, he strode to the center of the MacKinnon courtyard with his shoulders back, the click of his boot heels reminding him of his heritage. While he knew he didn't stand a chance, his innate stubbornness took stock of his surroundings.

There were less than a dozen men around him.

Four bloodied MacKinnon swords lay on the ground in odd places. In fact, he knew exactly which one belonged to his sire—the one on the platform in the middle with the green emerald in the hilt.

As he surveyed the area, he had to fight to keep the strongest memory from bringing a grin to his face, something he didn't wish to let his accusers know—the one move he'd done long ago to the entertainment of his father—the storage of his slinger as a young age. There it sat in the pocket he'd built into the stone platform.

His brother Craeg had laughed at him, calling him a fool and a dreamer. Then he'd punched him twice for being daft, as Craeg had said.

His youngest brother Boyd had laughed so hard he'd fallen to his knees. But Boyd loved to laugh about anything and everything.

Young Symon had lifted his chin and said to his sire, "This could be the one weapon I need one day."

His father had loved to laugh at his odd conjectures, but not this one. Instead, he'd narrowed his gaze at his son and quietly announced, "Ye could be right. Ye lads will never touch that slinger. Ye'll leave it there, understood?"

Craeg got that look on his face that his father recognized, the one that said he would do the opposite of what he was told. "Craeg, if I see ye near that spot, I'll flay yer backside in front of everyone."

Symon had glowed with pride. His father had agreed with him, something that didn't happen often.

Symon had been the one who didn't speak much, just plugged along at what he wished to do. His slinger had been first, practicing on animals in the forest, before he honed his skills as a swordsman. Though his sire had always said Craeg was the best, Symon knew better.

But Craeg followed his sire around so often that he often bumped into him, while Symon had insisted he was his own man.

To the chagrin of his father, though on occasion, he'd seen a light of approval in his sire's eyes when the brothers argued. His mother had never approved of his silent ways, but his sire did on occasion. His mother always wished to know what he was thinking.

No one could ever figure him out.

Craeg had spent all his time chasing light-skirts and visiting festivals, winning awards with his swordsmanship. To Symon, those awards meant naught. To him, the only person he wished to beat was himself.

Always do better. That was his motto for life. After all, he knew someday becoming Chieftain of Clan MacKinnon would fall on his shoulders. Craeg could do whatever he wished to do.

Now his sire was gone, that he knew for sure. He'd seen Boyd go down hard after taking a sword to his belly, and Craeg had been struck in his leg, a wound that was surely mortal. His mother? He'd never seen her body for certain but Finn had. She must have been killed right after his father.

Right after Symon had been knocked out.

Malcolm Chisolm led him to the platform in the middle of the courtyard where Malcolm's father and brother now stood, a handful of guards laughing and jesting around the periphery.

They tied his hands behind him, making sure he'd be unable to retaliate.

The chieftain asked, "Where are the barrels of whisky? Do no' give me some small one. I found the nearly empty one in yer cellar. It was mighty fine, but I want it all."

"I dinnae know what ye're looking for. I've been forced to drink mead for a long time." Symon looked that bastard in the eye, and it gave him great pleasure to look down on the lying brute. Symon stood taller than most men, and in times like these, he was grateful.

Malcolm punched him in the belly, and he doubled over with an oof. It was time to make up his mind. Would he try to fight or just let the bastards kill him?

"Ye are aware that it was yer drunkenness that allowed us in, do ye no', Symon? Because of ye, Malcolm came in the front entrance and let our men in the back, just because ye had to take yer horse for a short ride in the middle of the night and told yer guards to leave the portcullis open for a quarter hour. 'Twas all the time we needed.

If yer sire were here, I'd tell him it was entirely yer fault."

Symon made no comment simply because he couldn't. He didn't recall that part of the night. His head was too daft from drink. It sounded as if it could be true, but would he ever know for sure?

Was his sire's death his fault? And his brothers and sister? And his mother?

"What did you do to my sister?" He adored Alicia. She was honest and hard-working, and they had a relationship that was far better than any with his brothers. Boyd was improving, but he was the youngest male and had much to learn. Craeg? He was a lazy arse.

Ewart Chisholm, the middle son, said, "I had a nice night with that one. She's got some nice titties. She was a feisty one, but I had her all settled down before I gave her to Tavish, and he got mad at her and smashed her head against the wall. Just like a pumpkin exploding. I've ne'er seen the like before. She was spirited." He guffawed and slapped his knee, the guards joining in.

His sister was the one person in his family that he loved unconditionally. Alicia had a heart of gold but could fight like any man.

But she couldn't fight off ten men. The thought of her death set another fire deep in his belly. Her death and whatever other hell they subjected her to.

"This is yer last chance to talk, MacKinnon. If ye dinnae tell us where yer jewels and yer liquid gold are, we'll kill the lad in front of ye."

Finn MacKinnon was dragged forward by two guards, a look on his face that was a mix of fear and anger, as any young laddie would be.

But something else fired him up more than anything.

There was a bruise on Finn's face.

Malcolm then made his biggest mistake. He strode over to the lad and punched him directly in the belly.

A big bully—just what he detested.

Symon vowed to kill every one of them.

CHAPTER TWO

JOHANNA MOR MURRAY climbed out of bed with a groan, quickly stifling it so no one would overhear her pain. Being under the weather would get her nowhere, only more fists or slaps to her sore body. She did her ablutions quickly, then did her best to manage her long thick hair into a neat plait, though it was intent on being unruly this day.

She sighed, thoughts of better days, of a finer life, floating through her mind fleetingly. It wouldn't do for her to waste her time dreaming. It was time to get to work.

It wasn't her usual work that caused all the groans, but the extra work she'd been forced to do at the end of the day. She'd had to move all the furniture from Rohesia's chamber to another empty one, and she'd been forced to move all the chests and chairs on her own. The only item she hadn't had to move was the four-poster bed.

She'd fallen flat on her face at one point to the entertainment of the sisters. The wicked duo she called them.

How she hated her present situation.

Ever since her parents had chosen to sell her to the Smalleys, her life had taken a turn for the worst. Three years ago, Johanna's father had hurt his back and could no longer work as a blacksmith. She had been too small and young to help at the smithy and her parents said they had no choice but to sell her to work as a housemaid to someone.

They'd chosen the Smalleys—miserable lot they were. Two sisters who thought they were princesses, one married with two daughters being brought up to be the same. The brother Henry was the one who bought Johanna but it was Rohesia's husband Barnard who seemed to have odd intentions for her, or so she often felt when the chill went up her spine whenever he was present.

Her mother and father had sold her, helped her pack her bags, and sent her off to the Smalleys. And she hadn't seen her parents since. Her father would call her ungrateful for all they'd done for her, but she wasn't feeling the least bit grateful at the moment.

But what was her alternative? She had no choice but to accept her lot in life. She was an only child, her parents had abandoned her, and now she was with a family who treated her like the dirt they tread their dainty slippers on.

Like the help she was.

Long ago, her mother had told her that someday she'd find a wonderful man to marry and she'd live a happy life, having bairns of her own. She often mentioned how they wished to have many grandbairns to love. But Johanna had led an isolated life, working alongside her mother at home. With no close neighbors or family nearby, Johanna had led a very sheltered, friendless life.

How could she marry when she met no one?

Voices called to her from the passageway outside her bedchamber. "Johanna, get yer lazy arse out of that bed. Ibb's raggies need to be changed. And she needs a bath, and Jocosa needs a bath too."

She had to admit she enjoyed their bairns more than the two sisters. Ibb was only a year and Jocosa was five winters.

"Coming. I'll be right there."

"Ye better be, or Barnard will give ye the stick." That was Aldreda, the nastier of the two. Barnard was Rohesia's husband and he made Johanna's skin crawl. He hadn't done what Aldreda threatened with the stick yet, but she feared it could come at any moment.

At any whim.

If she could find any way out of this position, she'd take it.

Without flinching.

Finn crumpled to the ground, crawling forward after he took the blow to his belly. Symon willed him to stand up, even moved toward him, but to his surprise, Finn outsmarted his captors.

As the fools laughed and jeered with each other, Finn took a small dagger from his trews and tossed it to Symon.

The only thing he needed.

Symon whirled around and caught the fine blade in his hand, righted it, and cut through the rope binding his hands, ignoring the blood now flowing from a nick made when he caught the dagger. That didn't matter. He had to stop them from hurting Finn and get them both away.

Fortunately, Finn's antics distracted the guards as he cried out, "Help me, please!" The lad kicked his attacker square in the bollocks, which sent all the guards after the lad.

That gave him the time he needed. Reaching into the hiding place he'd carefully designed long ago, he grabbed his slinger along with the rocks and struck three guards down as he ran toward his sire's sword.

Chaos reigned as Finn outran the small group of large and overweight guards. Symon kicked Malcolm to the ground from behind, then slammed the fool's head into the stone, knocking him out. He rolled off Malcolm and went at Ewart, kicking him in the bollocks, then when he bent over, his knee came up and caught the man in the forehead, snapping his head backwards.

Tavish turned and ran toward the line of guards chasing after the lad so Symon threw the dagger at him, catching him in the back of his neck. Symon dove for his father's sword and grabbed the hilt, feeling it heat in his hand as if it were glad to be back where it belonged, in the hands of a MacKinnon.

A guard grabbed Finn and held him upside down. "I'll kill ye, ye young fool."

"Let him go. You get one warning," Symon

bellowed as he approached the man who picked on a lad half his size.

"Why protect the lad? Just go. We'll let ye go and catch up with ye later. First, I'll beat this laddie for kicking me in my jewels." He grabbed his crotch with his free hand for emphasis.

Symon found another small dagger and flung it across the courtyard, catching the guard next to Finn's attacker in the belly, blood shooting everywhere. But the fool would not give up Finn. "I said go. I'm the head of the guards and the Chisolms are all gone, so leave us."

Symon turned around, surprised to see Malcolm and the other guards gone, but Ewart wasn't moving. What the hell kind of men were the Chisolms? The chieftain was nowhere in sight. "There's a problem with that. I dinnae like bullies, so I'll no' be leaving without him."

Three guards ran at him, their swords poised at him, but they were easily brought down. He swung his weapon with both hands and sent the first guard's weapon flying through the air. He struck the second guard with the flat of his blade, knocking him down face first. Symon stepped on him and used his sword to take the sword arm nearly off the next guard. "I said let him go!"

The last man stared at him wide-eyed as his compatriots deserted him. "You can have the wee termagant. Leave! This is Chisolm property now." He let the boy go, shoving him toward Symon.

Symon, with an eye on the remaining guard, reached out to the lad and pulled him urgently toward the stable yard behind them. "Grab whatever weapon you can find, lad, and a horse or two. We're off."

The pair grabbed a few odds and ends along the way, including a sack that had dropped out of Ewart's hands when he fell. "Come, Finn. The rest will return soon, and we need to find a horse and go."

"I hid one before. I'll show you. Just outside the back gate."

They raced around the castle and out the back door in the curtain wall, finding Finn's horse right where he said he left it. "This is one of our finest horses, Finn."

"I know. I like Nightmare. He's my favorite."

"Well done." He tossed the lad up and mounted behind him, heading off through the forest, unsure of where to go. There was only one place he had to stop before they headed far away.

"Where are ye headed, my lord?"

"Dinnae call me my lord. My name is Symon and 'tis what ye'll call me. I'm going to visit my wizened old friend deep in the forest at the back of MacGill land. I cannae go anywhere without warning him of all that has taken place."

"Ol' Kestar?"

"Aye, I must be sure he is safe from the Chisolms."

They arrived at the old healer's place in the forest two hours later. Symon was pleased he had not been followed. All along their quiet journey, he couldn't help but go over the words of the Chisolms, the words that had sent his gut to sinking in a way he never felt before. Malcolm had said that Symon had let them in. Was it true?

Were the deaths of all the people of Clan MacKinnon on his shoulders? He had no memory of what they accused him, but if true, he'd carry the guilt of his foolish actions for the rest of his life.

Did he dare ask Finn?

As if on cue, Finn said, "I heard what they said about you leaving in the middle of the night and leaving the gates open. I dinnae recall that at all. Why did ye do it?"

How could he answer? "I dinnae recall doing it either. If I did, I must have been full of whisky. Did ye see me at all, Finn?"

"Nay, and I was up late washing plaids. Mayhap he was lying to make ye feel bad," Finn offered, looking up at him.

Symon glanced back at the boy. "I hope ye're right."

What if it were true?

They arrived at the old healer's cottage well hidden in the forest and there was no sign of any other visitors. Finn hopped down and took the sacks of what they'd grabbed on their way out. "Know ye what is in any of these?"

He'd already taken the one full of coins and tucked them inside his sack since he recognized the black bag Ewart had been holding. It was the only thing of value he had left besides his sire's sword. "I dinnae. Why do ye no' go through them while I see if Kestar is here. If he isnae, we'll move on quickly."

Finn set the sacks on a big boulder and began

to check the contents of each. "Finn, I'm going around back to hide the horse." To his surprise, there were three other horses behind the cottage. As far as he knew, Kestar would only have one. He listened but heard no voices at all. Odd since it was near the supper hour.

Returning to the front, he kept his voice low. "Anything of value, Finn?"

Finn said, "A bag of dried meat, one had two MacKinnon plaids and the third had more daggers."

"Good, we'll not starve for a bit, will we? The plaids are good, now if we both had a change of tunic and trews…"

He placed the items in two sacks and tied them to the horse, then ushered Finn to the door. "There are three horses in the rear and I've no idea who else is here."

Symon opened the door slightly and peered around, searching for Chisolms or a sign of who the horses might belong to. There were only two people inside. Kestar sat at the center table with his head resting on the table. On a pallet near the hearth there appeared to be a patient covered with blankets that showed recent blood.

Who the hell could it be? Was it someone from Clan MacKinnon? If so, how had they gotten this far on their own?

"Kestar?"

The man jerked awake, his grizzled beard flying forward. His skin was like old leather from the many years in the sun, his hair gray and sparse, but his eyes were alert and wise.

"Symon, I'm so glad ye are here." Kester waved them inside. "Come in. Please hurry and close the door."

A moan came from the pallet, a voice definitely female. Someone he knew.

"Alicia?" He moved over to the pallet and knelt down, so hopeful to see his dear sister's face that he nearly shouted with excitement when her face popped out from under the blanket.

"Alicia, ye are…" He couldn't finish his sentence because he caught the bruises on her face. One from a slap, one black eye, numerous scratches across her beautiful skin. "Oh, Lici. I'm so sorry." He used the same nickname he'd used when she was a wee lassie, being six summers younger than his eight and twenty years. Memories of Ewart and his words about his sister returned to him. Beatings, hitting her head against stone. What kind of bastards beat women?

"Symon? Ye survived?" She pushed herself to a sitting position with a groan, then threw her arms around his neck. He held her as close as he dared while she broke into convulsive sobs, drenching his shoulder. He pulled a stool over, and once seated, he lifted her from the pallet and settled her on his lap.

"I am well." He set her head under his chin, giving her the chance to allow her emotions out freely, rubbing her back while she cried. "As well as can be expected. I have a wound on my leg that I'll let Kestar take a look at, but the rest will heal soon enough. Dinnae worry about me, sister. Ye have no idea how grateful I am to see ye."

When she was able to slow her tears, she pulled back and looked at his face. "Ye were beaten too."

"Dinnae worry about me. Who did this to ye?"

"Ewart. The bastard."

"Did he…"

"Nay. His father stopped him, but he beat me pretty well. Tavish wanted to join in, but he was also stopped. His father told them to bring me to Kestar. Who hurt ye?"

"The shorter question would be who didnae hit me? But dinnae fash, I am fine."

She looked around the cottage and asked, "The others? Mama? Craeg? Boyd? Papa?"

"They're all gone, lass. I'm so sorry."

"'Twas what I feared. Are ye certain?"

"I saw Chisolm sink his sword into Da myself. He is dead. I saw Craeg go down with a heavy wound to his leg and Boyd took a sword to his belly. And when I returned to the courtyard, I saw Mama's shawl over a body next to Da's. It had to be her."

Kestar said, "Belly wounds are usually fatal."

"Anyone else survive?" Alicia asked, her eyes ever hopeful.

"Finn and one horse we have. Finn and I spent the night in the dungeon. On the way out, I saw nae others, though we didnae have much chance to check. There were nae others in the dungeon or the courtyard. We just managed to get away, and 'tis all we have, but I thought we were alone. Others may have gotten away, but they would have had to get far away quickly. There were Chisolms everywhere, MacKinnon blood everywhere too." He let out a deep sigh of frustration at not being able to stop the slaughter. "I'm ecstatic to have found ye, dear sister," he said, kissing her forehead. "Many thanks to ye, Kestar, for taking care of her."

Kestar said, "Finn, sit down. All of ye, sit at the table and have some pottage I've been stewing in the hearth. We all need something warm in our bellies, and I have one loaf of bread from the other day at market. Feed yer bellies and then ye'll have to move on before the Chisolms come, I fear."

They settled with bowls of lamb pottage and ate heartily. "My apologies that I've nae whisky for ye, Symon, but I'm out."

"Nae apology necessary. I wouldn't drink it anyway. 'Tis in my past." He took a sip of the goblet of mead Kestar passed to him.

Kestar said, "Tell me what happened. I've heard little other than what Alicia has told me. And while ye're talking, stick that leg with the wound out here and I'll take a look at it. Bind it up for ye quickly."

"Chisolms came over the wall in the middle of the night and killed everyone they saw. Caught us off-guard, but we were also grossly outnumbered. I saw Fagan kill my father, saw both of my brothers go down along with so many of our guards. They didn't have the skills of the Chisolm guards."

"Did Craeg no' train them well enough?"

"Nay, he and the head of our guards both trained them, but no' well."

"Symon," Alicia interjected. "Ye were always

telling Papa they needed more training. Bryce tried, but he was never as skilled as ye. Why did he no' allow ye to do the training?"

"I never knew, Alicia. But our poor training cost us many lives." If he were to ever be in charge, the training would be entirely different.

"Why did they no' kill ye?" Kestar asked. "Ye are the heir to the chieftain."

"Because they expected me to tell them where the casks and barrels were held along with our jewels and coins. They found my sire's coin, but they wanted it all. They planned to use Finn to make me talk after they searched our castle well. But Finn had a different idea." He glanced at Finn with a nod and a smile.

Finn said, "I found a small dagger on a casing in the dungeon so I hid it in my trews, then tossed it to Symon once I was close enough." His wide grin told them everything. The lad was proud of his quick thinking. "Then he used it to cut through his bindings."

"Aye, thanks to Finn, we were able to fight our way out of their few guards. The rest must have been celebrating or burying the dead because they were nowhere in sight."

"So ye killed all the Chisolms?" Kestar asked, astonished.

"Nay, the chief got away. I shoved Malcolm to the ground and slammed his head against the stone, but I doubt he's dead. Ewart and Tavish were hurt, whether they survived is unknown."

"Och, Praise the Lord this day. God gave us each other in this terrible time," Kestar stated after he made the sign of the cross. "But what will ye do now?" Once he finished his prayer, he cleaned up Symon's leg and applied a poultice to the open wound to prevent festering.

"I've only just begun to think on it. Getting away was our only priority. I havenae gone that far yet in my head. I know this will no' be safe forever as they may come after me." Symon knew this was the biggest issue. He'd been thinking on it all the way here. Where could he and Finn go and be safe?

And now he had Alicia, and he suspected the Chisolms would come here to look for him knowing his sister was here.

"I dinnae know, but we cannae remain here. Alicia, can ye travel?"

"Aye. We must leave swiftly. They'll come for ye, Symon. Please. We must go."

Kestar said, "There. I've finished cleaning yer wound. Now we need to decide where ye are going. What have ye in mind, Symon?"

All three faces looked up at him with a hope that humbled him, but they were to be disappointed.

"I have nae idea."

"Do ye no' have a distant relation in the Highlands? What was his name? He was a fine friend of mine when I've visited. He's a kind and generous man. I'm sure ye'd be welcome there for a wee bit."

Symon pushed his thoughts to come up with the man Kestar referred to. He did hear his sire mention he had an old friend he had little to do with. Something about him becoming a recluse after losing his wife. "Gilbert? Aye, I recall his name, but our sire has no siblings. Gilbert was an old friend of Da's, one who had a rotten lot in life, but I cannae pull it from my mind. Do ye recall, Alicia?"

"Nay, I dinnae recall much about him. Mama mentioned him a few times, but she always referred to him as poor Gilbert. But I dinnae recall why."

Kestar snapped his fingers. "I remember. He lost his wife and bairn within a week or two of the child being born. He was so devastated that he moved out of his castle a year later and built a manor home, losing many of his clan mates. Though I know no' where they have gone."

Alicia said, "Please, Symon. We must go somewhere. I dinnae wish to see Ewart's face again."

Kestar looked at Symon, who nodded to him. "We'll go. But I cannae help but wonder if any other MacKinnons survived. And what of our king? If not for fear of being attacked, I would head to the king's castle in Edinburgh to report this attack. Chisolm will need to answer for what he's done to my clan."

Kestar explained, "Remember that ye are speaking of a man who lies about everything. My guess is he has planned this all along, that he's already sent a missive to our king saying ye provoked the attack or some other scathing falsehood. First ye need to protect the three of ye. They'll no' bother me and I'll return to see if there are others. Did ye pass any along the way?"

"Nay," Symon replied, rubbing his hands together. "Not a soul. Naught was moving inside the castle wall except Chisolms. I fear they killed them all."

Finn sat up, "But some were gone. One family was visiting in the Highlands. When they return, they'll no' know what happened. What then?"

Symon clasped Finn's shoulder. "We must move on to protect ourselves. If there are others who survived, they'll no' show themselves near the Chisolms for fear of death. Our only alternative is to head to the Highlands, find old Gilbert, and hope we can stay with him until we figure out what our choices are."

Kestar said, "Ye speak wisely, Symon. I'll travel with ye but when I return, I'll uncover the truth of the situation."

"Ye said ye've met Gilbert?"

"Aye, Gilbert Morrigan. I stayed with him a few years ago when I traveled through the Highlands. I believe I can find him again. He's no' far off the main path."

Symon stood up and said, "I think we must go while we still can. Are ye able, sister?"

"Aye."

"Then we're off to the Highlands. Finn, ready the horses."

Finn bolted out of his chair with a cheer and raced out the door.

Kestar shook his head with a smile. "To be young again. I'm glad the lad found ye, Symon."

"We've been blessed this day. I hope all improves from this day forward."

Now if Symon could only believe his own words.

CHAPTER THREE

KESTAR SAID, "I'M ready."

"Good," Symon said. "Because I think the only place we'll be safe is deep in the Highlands."

He helped Alicia to get dressed, wrapping her mantle around her carefully so as not to cause her any pain. "I see yer horse in the back. Who do the other two belong to?" Symon asked. "They look like MacKinnon horses, though I didnae look closely."

"They found their way here. They verra well could be MacKinnon horses."

"They are our horses, I just checked," Finn added as he came back inside. "Chisolms set many of ours free. Stole some but the rest they sent away."

"Do ye recall anything, Alicia?"

"Nay, I dinnae awaken until I was on the pallet."

Kestar said, "Leave it be, Symon. Probably a blessing. Ewart threw her on my doorstep, then left without a word. I saw him leaving."

"Since they left Alicia here and they are still after our treasures, we cannae afford to wait. We must leave immediately. We have a few hours of daylight left, so I believe we must take advantage of that time. I hope we can find Gilbert, and I hope he is no' too far into the Highlands. I am pleased ye have agreed to travel with us, Kestar."

"I'll be glad to avoid the Chisolms for a bit. I'll pack up and meet ye outside, Symon. We must hurry."

"Finn, come with me." They stepped outside, then checked the horses in the back. "I didnae get a good look at them." He moved over to the two horses, both saddled with MacKinnon saddles. "Finn, is this no' Dark Star?" He moved over to the one mare who acted unsettled, but she was with two stallions.

"It is! Alicia will be so pleased. How did she get here?"

Symon smiled, holding his hand out to the black horse with white markings on her face, the top looking much like the shape of a star. She nuzzled him for a treat. "I have naught for ye, sweet lady. But I'll find ye something if ye carry my sister safely into the Highlands." He leaned in to whisper sweet words in her ear and she neighed softly.

Finn said, "Symon, ye always have been magical with animals. How do ye do it? Will ye teach me?"

Symon stood back and said, "Aye, I'll do what I can, but 'tis all about kindness to animals." He patted Dark Star's withers, then moved over to the other horse. "And this fine stallion was one my sire liked, but he's just a wee laddie. He'll be good and strong for the trip into the Highlands."

Symon spoke softly to all three horses, rubbing them in various places as they whinnied their satisfaction to him. "Finn, do ye speak Gaelic?"

"Nay. Do ye?"

"I do. I learned much from Kestar. We'll teach ye."

"Why?"

"Because Gaelic is the common language in the Highlands. Fill a few sacks of oats from the grain barrel. I'll see if Kestar is ready to leave yet. We'll need some foodstuffs and other items." Symon headed back toward the front of the cottage, beginning to feel a wee bit of hope.

"Aye, I'll learn. I'm excited!" The lad hopped into the air, but then froze at the sound of a growl. His eyes widened as he turned his head slowly to look behind him. "Symon?"

Symon took two careful steps toward the sound, enough to peer through the trees. He chuckled and said, "Where have ye been, Hunter? And I see ye have yer best lady with ye. Are ye protecting her? Is that why ye growl so? Come, Shadow."

Finn was dumbfounded, if he could tell by his expression of surprise. "How did they end up here? I do no' understand how they could be at the same place we are."

"My guess is Alicia was riding Dark Star, lying across her, until Ewart took her off to lay her on the step of Kestar's cottage. Ewart left the horse because they're no' fond of female horses. And the dogs probably caught scent of us along the way and followed us. We just never noticed them. Dogs have an uncanny way of finding their owners, mark my words, they either caught our scent or Alicia's."

Finn spun around and shrieked with delight. "Why were ye growling at me, Hunter?" The deerhounds were both gray with wiry hair, but their tails let them know they were as pleased to see a familiar face as Finn was. Hunter was a head taller than Shadow, but they were faithful hunting dogs of Clan MacKinnon.

"Probably because there was a horse they did no' recognize. They're fine now. We have a couple of hunters to go along with us. 'Tis a fine time to have the dogs join us."

Finn whispered, "Hunter keeps me warm in the cold nights."

"Aye, hounds put out much heat, they do. Come, we'll help gather all we need. We have nae time to waste." Symon headed back to the front of the cottage but then stopped for a moment to turn back to the boy, embarrassed because he didn't know the answer to his question, but he knew he needed to know the truth. "Yer parents, Finn. I know ye lost them, but how long ago? And how?"

"They both died of the fever two winters ago. So did my wee sister. She was just a bairn."

He clasped Finn's shoulder and said, "My sympathies. I know now exactly how ye feel."

Finn said, "But we can make a new clan, can we no', Symon?"

Symon stared up at the gray sky, the sun dropping in the horizon. "My hope is we'll come back to reclaim what is ours. But if we must, we shall rebuild. Wherever we can. The Highlands will work if we must."

Three hours later, the group slowed their horses as they headed north, waiting for Kestar to assess the area they were in. "Somewhere off this path is another healer I've met. She's a fine one and she lives with her daughter. She has two cottages so she can allow anyone who needs healing to spend the night. If we are fortunate enough, she'll no' have anyone occupying it and we can use it for one night. These bones are too old for the ground. A little farther north, I think."

Symon glanced over at his sister. "Alicia, ye'll ride with me on the morrow."

His sister, barely managing to stay upright, nodded her agreement. "I'm tired, Symon. Are we close?"

"Say the word and I'll lift ye onto my horse."

"I can continue a wee bit more. Lead the way, Kestar."

They followed the old healer along the path for a little longer, Symon moving his gaze from the horizon and the setting sun, back to his sister. He'd have to be ready to catch her if she weakened. She was a strong lass. One he was proud of, especially when she took on archery. Their father had argued about a lass learning such a skill, but their mother had convinced him it would do Alicia no harm.

Part of him wished to go back and fight. Gather whatever men he could and return to regain his heritage—his clan—his castle. He had to constantly tell himself that his priority at the moment was the safety of the three he was with. He would bring his dearest, injured sister to shelter along with a young lad who probably had saved his life with one smart move and a dagger. And Kestar? He had taken care of his sister. He owed him, as well.

Nay. Now was not the time to play hero and go on the attack on the Chisolms. His day would come, but he had other more important matters to attend first. After all, what was his castle without his clan?

"There," Kestar declared, pointing at a path heading west. "'Tis down that path."

The odd group of two men, a lad, and a lass, four horses, and two deerhounds headed down the path. Finn nearly bounced in his seat. "I smell the smoke from the hearth."

"Good, because I'm cold," Alicia said.

When they came into the clearing, Symon had to admit it was a much more pleasing picture than Kestar's cottage. Two huts sat side by side, a path of stones leading from one to the other and also between the two cottages. The front of the house held a large bed of flowers and herbs, the fragrances calling to him, making his belly rumble.

Kestar chuckled. "I feel the same. Lady Ella is quite the cook. I smell beef stew is my guess. And some baked berries."

"Is she a noblewoman?" Alicia asked.

"Nay, I've always called her Lady Ella. Her

daughter Florie is around five and ten, I believe. She tends the herb garden. And they have a fine vegetable garden behind the cottages plus fruit trees here and there. Her husband died from a fall off a horse two years ago. No one bothers them because they are so skilled. Come, I'll introduce ye."

Symon dismounted and then lifted Alicia down. "I'll carry ye in if ye need, sister."

"Nay, I can walk inside."

The front door opened and a tall willowy woman with brown hair plaited to her waist stepped out. "Kestar? Is that ye up this far in the north?"

"Aye, we're in need of housing for the night, at least for the lass, if ye can abide us, Lady Ella." He dismounted and tied his horse to a nearby tree branch off to the periphery of the property.

"No one is in the cottage next door. Ye may use that for as long as ye like. Ye know ye are always welcome." Her daughter stood behind her peering over her shoulder. She was a wee bit shorter than her mother, but a lovely lass.

Lady Ella took a few steps before her gaze settled on Alicia. If Symon were to guess, as a skilled healer, she knew right away that the lass was in need of tending. "Kestar, why do ye men no' take care of the horses, feed them. There's water in that barrel and buckets on the side of the house. I have a large bag of oats inside the small stable. Take what ye need. I'll take the lass inside. In fact, mayhap ye men can stay in that cottage and we lasses will stay in mine. I have finer accommodations here than the other one."

Symon looked at his sister, who breathed a sigh of relief. "Will that suit ye? Kestar trusts her."

"Aye, as long as ye have a meal with me." Her knees buckled so Symon scooped her into his arms and nodded to Lady Ella.

"If ye'll lead me inside, my lady."

"Florie, show him in while I speak with Kestar for a moment." Lady Ella waved her daughter inside while she held the door for Symon.

Florie said, "'Tis a chair with a back and arms near the hearth. She may set there. It has a soft cushion on it, and she'll be nice and warm. And there are extra furs and blankets in the basket next to the fireside."

Symon settled her in the chair, and Florie found a woolen blanket to cover Alicia's legs. He hadn't noticed his poor sister was shivering. "I'll bank the fire for ye."

"Then please go, Symon. I have needs."

Symon quickened his pace then hurried outside. He hadn't even thought of the fact that they hadn't stopped yet. How was she going to be able to tend her needs on the morrow?

He would worry about that later, instead hurrying outside after planting a kiss on Alicia's forehead, who gave him a wee push. "Go, Symon."

Symon stepped outside, not surprised to see Kestar and Lady Ella deep in a conversation. He joined them and asked, "What have ye heard, my lady?"

She clasped his hand with her two, a move that surprised him, but he didn't pull away. The touch was appreciated for some odd reason. "All are saying the Chisolms have killed all the MacKinnons. I'm pleased to see ye and yer sister have survived. She's quite a beauty with hair dark as night, and I would bet that beneath all her bruises she has beautiful skin and fine bone structure."

"She's a lovely lass, aye, she is. She looks much like her younger brother."

"Is the lad tending the animals a brother?"

"Nay, Finn's a clan mate who survived. He's a fine young lad. Lost his parents two years ago. Has anyone come by looking for us?"

"Nay. We are only known to the local villagers. We stay hidden as much as we can, but I was called to deliver a bairn. I heard talk there. Ye are welcome to stay as long as ye like, but from what Kestar has told me, I would guess ye'll need to keep moving north. He's told me yer plan briefly. I was paid with a large sack of oat seed for the delivery, more than I can ever use. I'd be happy to give ye half the bag to take with ye. See if ye can grow some before autumn is here. I have plenty of vegetable seed to share with ye, so I'll have Florie sort the seeds and label them this eve. Squash, peas, beans, turnips. Ye'll need to eat."

"T'would be greatly appreciated. Finn can help. Anything ye need done, I'm happy to help. I'll chop some wood before we eat, if ye have enough food to share."

"Always." She patted his hand and let go. "Come, I'll show ye the cottage where ye both can freshen up. Then I'll check on Florie and yer sister. It looks like ye have a few cuts that could use some tending, Chief MacKinnon. Aye? Along with a larger wound on yer leg?"

He stared at Lady Ella, simply because of her name for him. He was the chieftain of his clan. What remained of it. "I am fine, my lady. Once I leave our things in the cottage, I'll cut yer wood." He whistled for Finn, who came running.

Lady Ella led them to the second cottage, a bit smaller than the other. "We have a hearth and a table, but not much else. Two chairs and a few stools, but we have two chambers to sleep in. Each one has two pallets." She opened the door and stepped inside.

The hearth sat to the left with two chairs in front of it, a basket of blankets next to the hearth. It had the feminine touches that Kestar's hut lacked—dried flowers about, cushions on the chairs, two books on a chest of drawers.

"Two bedchambers with two beds. 'Tis an odd combination, Lady Ella. Why?" Kestar stopped to turn to her while Symon went to work on a fire in the hearth.

"One pallet for the patient and one for the family member tending them. Usually they are brought by someone. And I often have two patients. And if a woman is delivering, she can be here for a long time. I try to go to their homes, but if two are ready at the same time, I bring them here."

"Ye are a wise woman, Lady Ella."

Symon took the two sacks he brought in and

set them on the chest in one bedchamber. Then he left to cut wood. Finn bolted inside just as Symon was about to leave. "I have Alicia's sack and mine."

"Put them in that second bedchamber. Ye'll sleep in the other pallet with me, and Kestar will have the first bedchamber. I'll bring Alicia her sack when we go to supper."

Lady Ella came up behind them as Finn darted to set the sacks down. He held the door for Lady Ella and she stepped outside. "My lady."

"Aye?" she asked, stopping to turn to him.

"I dinnae know exactly how badly my sister was hurt. Would ye please ask her the hard questions a brother can no'?"

"I'll take good care of yer sister, Symon. Dinnae worry." Then she strode off to the other cottage. "Supper in about an hour." She waved to him and closed the door behind her. "Whatever wood ye are able to cut in that short time will be greatly appreciated."

Finn came out, not surprised to find the dogs resting at Symon's feet. "I'll finish tending the horses. Ye are cutting wood?"

He couldn't stop staring at the cottage where his sister sat. What exactly had happened to her?

"Aye."

Kestar stuck his head out and said, "I'm in need of a wee rest before we eat."

Symon nodded and waved at him.

He had three people to take care of now. Three people, two dogs, and four horses. And mayhap two women if they were attacked. His hand settled on the hilt of his sword.

He had a feeling that all his practicing with his sword was going to pay off.

CHAPTER FOUR

A BOUT AN HOUR later, Symon stepped inside the cottage feeling refreshed. He'd taken a bucket of water and cleaned himself up to the best of his ability under the circumstances. How he wished he had a nearby loch to jump into to take the stench of death from his nostrils. They had survived something very few people could understand.

Lady Ella had a large trestle table in the center of the room. The hearth was at the back of the hut with a grouping of chairs in front of it. To the left sat three chests with broad tops, one looked to carry a healer's potions, the next linens and tools, and the third carried herbs and food items. The pot hanging over the fire in the hearth set his belly to rumbling because the smell was as aromatic as any he'd ever smelled before.

Alicia sat near the fire, but didn't get up, staying huddled under a soft blue blanket. "I know ye've caught the aroma, Symon. It smells mighty fine. Lady Ella has been teaching me about herbs and spices that can also be used in cooking." She picked up a pretty sack of dark green fabric. "I already have cuttings, seeds, and bags of ointments to bring along on our journey."

Florie said, "Ye can start yer own place. We have much to share."

They settled at the table, Symon assisting Alicia to her feet. She managed better than he expected. She glanced up at him with an apologetic look. "I just needed a wee rest. And the bed I have is a mattress of lavender and heather with many furs and pillows. I'll sleep like a wee bairn this night. I'll be able to travel on the morrow, I promise."

"I'm glad to hear it. We'll do what we must to get ye to the Highlands with us." They took their seats while Florie filled bread trenchers with beef stew full of carrots and turnips. Two loaves of dark crusty bread sat at either end of the table.

Finn looked to another side table. "What are those?"

"Berry tarts for everyone after we finish the meal. They are nice to eat by the fire," Lady Ella said.

Florie whispered, "Mama's best."

They had a pleasant meal and Symon had to do all he could not to ask for two more trenchers of the delectable stew. "What are the flavorings ye use, Lady Ella?" he asked. "I've no' tasted stew this flavorful."

"Just spices from my garden: parsley, rosemary, a wee bit of sage. Salt that comes fresh from the sea. Ye approve?"

Symon and Finn both answered with vigor. "Aye. 'Tis most delicious."

Lady Ella gave Symon and Finn a wee bit more but the others refused. After they settled around the fire, the conversation they needed to have began. "How much farther to Gilbert's land, Kestar?" Finn asked. "Will we be there by the morrow?"

"I'm not exactly sure," Kestar mumbled, pulling on his grizzled beard until he had the end a fine point. "'Tis north of Perth. Just north of Dunkeld, I believe."

Finn looked to Symon who quickly answered, "I dinnae know. I've no' been to the Highlands. Traveled to Edinburgh, Glasgow, and London, but no' into the Highlands. And never to Gilbert's home. While he was a close friend of Da's, we never met him."

Lady Ella said, "I've traveled that way many times. Depending on the weather, I would say if you traveled around Perth and straight through Dunkeld without stopping, you should be there before nightfall if ye leave early enough. If the weather slows ye, ye may wish to find an inn at Perth."

Kestar said, "I know one that has been suitable before, but if we leave early enough, and I believe we must to stay out of the reach of the Chisolms, I think we can make it before dusk. While I dinnae mind a quick stop in Dunkeld, I think it best if we dinnae stay long."

Alicia said, "Symon, ye willnae worry about me. I will make it half the day on my own horse, then I shall ride with ye."

"Ye'll ride with me all day." Symon couldn't believe his sister would think she could ride on her own. Her situation was still tenuous at best.

"Nay, I willnae ride with ye until high sun. We must move quickly. After all I've endured, riding sweet Dark Star on my own willnae be difficult. We cannae afford to move slowly."

Lady Ella said, "She's a strong lass and she'll tell ye when she's in need. I've checked her thoroughly and she has no broken bones, no fever, and I've carefully dressed any wounds that needed tending."

Kestar said, "Then we're settled. We leave at first light and hope we make it at least to Perth by nightfall."

Symon had no argument. How he prayed the Chisolms would not find them.

★★★

They left at first light, and Symon was pleased to see the sparkle back in Alicia's eyes. She managed Dark Star like she had no injuries, and the mare was pleased to have her usual mistress.

They met no impediments to their journey, even made it past Perth without any delays.

"Know ye the way from here, Kestar?"

"The only way I know goes directly through Dunkeld, but I preferred to stop to pick up foodstuffs and anything else I needed at the market when I have traveled before. Herbs are plentiful there and ye can find shoemakers, glovers, and tailors aplenty between Perth and Dunkeld."

"I propose we make a quick stop to get some

fresh baked goods and some meat pies. How far is Gilbert's land from there?"

"Less than an hour. We can return any time for boots for winter, whatever else we shall need."

They arrived in Dunkeld with time to spare. Once they found an inn to feed them, Symon and Finn made their way to the town stables and left their horses there while Kestar and Alicia went inside the inn to warm up. Alicia had held up well, so he had no more worries about her.

They left their horses and the hounds at the stable, Symon paying for their feed and care. He was about to cross the street when he heard a woman's scream followed by the loud laughter of others. Curious as to what had happened, Symon made his way down a side-street to follow the cacophony, surprised to see a woman face down in the dirt, her packages tossed about her, and another woman kicking her while she was down.

The laughter came from the aggressive woman doing the kicking and a woman standing next to her with two lassies. The older lassie ran over to kick the woman who was down, then giggled and ran away.

Every time the poor woman tried to stand, she was shoved down again. There were two men standing in front of a shop, and they appeared to be with the group of women.

Two big bullies laughing with two bigger bullies.

He said to Finn, "I'll be back in a moment."

When he thought about it later, he might wonder why he needed to get involved, but he knew there was no thought in his movement at all. It was instinct.

Protect the weak.

He marched into the middle of the growing crowd now watching the chaos, oblivious to whatever the kicking lass was going to do. Some told her to kick harder, fueling her cruelty, while others told her to stop.

He wasn't interested in that fool.

He marched over to the lass on the ground and held his hand out to her. Her attacker yelled, "Here now, leave her be. She dropped the packages."

"Then don't make her burden so heavy," he retorted. The woman attempted to kick him, but he was faster, grabbing her booted foot while it was about to kick his bollocks. He held firm and the woman fell to the ground, now bellowing and shouting for a sheriff to arrest him. He let her boot go and reached for the woman on the ground, setting his hands under her arms and lifting her to her feet.

The fury in her eyes caught him, but only for a second. What caught him more was the beauty of the woman who'd been accosted.

Blue eyes locked onto his, her light brown hair falling out of her plait, the soft curls making a halo around her face. Her porcelain skin was dotted with dirt, but even that could not prevent her beauty from shining through. She lifted her chin with a rare sense of pride and said, "Many thanks to you but I can take care of myself."

She was English, taller than he expected as she was up to his nose, no small feat for a woman. And feisty. Proud. Strong.

But those characteristics could not hide the misting in her eyes at being ridiculed in front of a crowd. Symon knew that even the toughest could fail when it seemed the world was against them. He had an inkling she was going through emotions similar to the ones he had felt when he was led through the courtyard and the bystanders spat upon him in a fury.

"I'm sure ye can, my lady, but I dinnae like bullies. And she is a bully as are the others watching."

"Pick up my packages," the woman bellowed, her hands locked on her ample hips. "You've probably ruined half of them. They'll come out of your wages."

"Well," she retorted, spinning around to face her attacker. "Since I do not receive any wages, I do not know how you will accomplish that, but see if you can. Will it please you more?"

"You have a mighty sharp tongue for a woman who is naught more than a noble woman's maid," the older man behind her attacker said.

Symon's fury knew no bounds. He stalked over to the man and said, "Ye think this was the right way to treat her? I think ye must treat yer dogs better. What in hellfire is wrong with ye that ye allow yer women to treat another so?"

"Close your mouth and mind your business, not ours. Go on your way."

He turned away from the fools and moved back to the woman, now busy picking up packages. "What is yer name?"

For some reason, he had to know. He'd never been greatly attracted to a specific woman before, not like this. Oh, he'd recognized keen minds and pretty faces, but this woman was different. She had a core of steel, if he were to guess. Nothing could bring her down.

"It really does not concern you." She picked up the last package, brushed the dirt off the outside of it, and tucked it inside a larger bag. "Again, thank you for what you've done, but I must be on my way."

The crowd began to disband, people going in different directions.

"Please. Yer name."

"Johanna, hurry your arse and get the packages into the cart."

He smiled and she glared at him.

"Until we meet again, Johanna." He smiled and gave a small bow, but she spun on her boot heel and moved toward the cart, never looking back.

But he did. He couldn't tear his gaze away from her.

CHAPTER FIVE

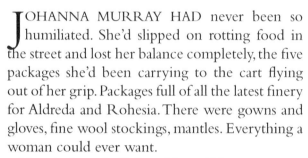

JOHANNA MURRAY HAD never been so humiliated. She'd slipped on rotting food in the street and lost her balance completely, the five packages she'd been carrying to the cart flying out of her grip. Packages full of all the latest finery for Aldreda and Rohesia. There were gowns and gloves, fine wool stockings, mantles. Everything a woman could ever want.

How jealous she'd found herself for a moment. Until she realized what they truly had were things she did not want. She didn't want the inconsiderate slob of a brother or husband the two had, nor would she prefer to be born into a family such as the Smalleys.

They spent their lives ridiculing, gossiping, and picking on others. No, she was not jealous of them.

But she still could be affected by the situation she was just forced to endure. Hurt feelings galore, plus she was embarrassed, humiliated, and sore.

The cruel bitch Aldreda had kicked her backside over and over again until she was nearly in tears. Every time she attempted to stand, Aldreda kicked her again. Her best gown was now covered in dirt and mud, maybe even some horse droppings mixed in here and there. How she'd like to push Aldreda's face into a pile of horse droppings.

Disgusted. That was another word she could use to describe her experience. And to have a man come to her rescue was even more embarrassing.

She hated her life.

She squared her shoulders and carefully arranged the packages in the cart. Aldreda's sister Rohesia said, "Who was that man who assisted ye? How do ye know him?" Her glare was something Johanna would love to put her fist to, but since she was a lady, she would not.

"I do not know him."

"Too handsome for the likes of ye. A nice strong Scotsman for ye, Aldreda." Rohesia was the prettier of the two. Both had mousy brown hair, one prone to frizzing and the other stick straight. It was Aldreda's pointed nose that kept her from being marriage material, if Johanna were to guess. Her eyes were dark, and her hips were ample, something she needed because her fists settled there often.

If Aldreda set her sights on the tall Scot, that could prove interesting.

"I'll have to find out exactly who he is. I like them tall and dark," she said with a wink to her sister.

Johanna moved around the cart, giving herself the opportunity to subtly steal another look at the man who'd rescued her. She'd noticed how handsome he was, long dark hair curling when it met his shoulders, and green eyes that had emblazoned themselves into her soul for a moment's time. His shoulders were the broadest she'd ever seen, and the swing of his sword acted as notice to any observer that one would not attack him easily.

She turned away, regretting her stare. But what good would it do her to be interested in any man? She was indentured to the Smalleys and they promised to betroth her to someone of their choice. Another deal made for coin, if she were to guess. Henry Smalley would betroth her to a man she had not met yet, without consulting her at all.

Two moons from now she could find herself away from the Smalleys, living with a daft man of their choice. She had nothing to look forward to at all.

Or for all she knew, she could end up dead six moons from now at the hands of her husband. For some reason, that thought did not bother her.

Aldreda said, "I must learn his name. I'll be betrothed to the man soon, ye can wager on that one, Rohesia." Even Aldreda's laugh was much like the cackle of a witch.

She couldn't help but wonder if she had warts somewhere on her body with hairs growing from them.

Now she had a reason to get to know the man who'd helped her.

She needed to warn him. Aldreda was a bitch.

They made it to Gilbert's house shortly after dark. The bullies were the only thing that slowed their trip, but Symon did not regret his actions at all.

Kestar introduced them all to his friend, Gilbert Morrigan. "Gilbert is a fine friend. Do ye recall any of the MacKinnon's, Gilbert?"

"Aye, if ye are the bairns of my good friend, Ronan. I havenae seen him in years, but I havenae gone far, ever since…well, enough for now. What brings ye all to the Highlands?"

"Greetings to ye," Symon began. "We are pleased to meet ye. My sire spoke highly of ye, but I am sorry to tell ye he was killed by a warring clan a few days ago. Clan MacKinnon was attacked in the middle of the night by Clan Chisolm, and I was witness to Fagan Chisolm putting a blade in my father's chest, killing him instantly. Alicia is my sister, but we also lost our mother and two brothers. We come to ye for help, as we dinnae know where else to go."

"Praise be to God, Symon, but I am here to help ye in any way I can. Yer sire was a fine friend of mine, and 'tis my honor to assist ye. But for now, please come in, bring all yer guests inside to warm yerselves. I have a blazing fire in the main chamber that I'm sure the young lady will find comforting." He ushered the group inside, calling out to a housemaid to assist with their outerwear.

The house was not truly a castle, but a large manor home. There were a couple of outbuildings surrounding the home. The stable, mayhap a buttery or just something for storage, he wasn't sure. But the holding was well-kept and the servants were many and very accommodating. Comparing this place to the abuse he witnessed in the center of Dunkeld saddened him. What could poor Johanna's life be like living in that situation all day long?

He focused on his present company, a task more difficult than he guessed it would be simply because of a pair of luscious pink lips that had caught his eye.

Would he ever see her again? If so, under the right conditions, he hoped to be able to get to know her better. Much better. He forced himself to come back to his present situation, luscious lips now cast aside.

Gilbert Morrigan was much younger than Kestar. He knew the man had lost his wife and daughter at a young age, and never remarried. Once they were all settled around the hearth, Gilbert asked the serious questions.

"Tell me how I can help ye all, besides a few nights' lodgings. I dinnae receive visitors often, so I am not always aware of all that goes on around me. Please tell me again what happened to Clan MacKinnon. I understand ye lost yer parents and siblings, but what of the rest of the clan? And where are the Chisolms now?"

Kestar cleared his throat and the other three waited patiently for him to explain. Symon would help eventually, but he felt the beginning needed to come from Kestar.

"Gilbert, these are all that remain of Clan MacKinnon that we know. Clan Chisolm attacked the MacKinnons, killing nearly all their clan mates. One of the sons dropped a beaten Alicia on my doorstep, so I helped where I could. Symon and Finn came to me the next day because they'd escaped the dungeon and were running from the Chisolms. They have no home and nowhere to go. They are fine people, my friends, and I thought to help them out. Waiting at my cottage would surely have caused their death as the Chisolms were intent on finding Symon. He is heir to the chieftain, and the Chisolms wish for him to reveal all the MacKinnon treasures."

Symon added, "Treasures they havenae found yet, and they willnae be able to find the jewels or the casks of whisky. But they arenae prepared to give up on their pursuit of our perceived wealth yet. Fortunately, anything we have was well-hidden by my sire."

"Clan Chisolm ye say? Word has no' traveled here but I suspect 'twill soon enough. My greatest sympathies for all ye've lost. Symon, ye are the chieftain's eldest son? Ye say ye saw yer father killed, what about yer mother and yer brothers?"

"My mother's body was next to my sire's. My two brothers were both seriously wounded, and I've not seen them since. As far as I know, Alicia and I are the only ones remaining of the chieftain's family. Finn worked in the stables and hid himself well, so I invited him to join us. He has no family left other than clan mates."

"Finn, a stable lad is a fine job. Symon, ye and yer sister were also beaten by Chisolms? I see ye both carry bruises."

Symon nodded. "We've come to the Highlands for safety until we can decide what to do next. We dinnae know if the Chisolms will continue their pursuit. Mayhap the best plan would be to travel to Edinburgh to speak to our king, but at this point, I feel that would be risking our lives. We lost all our guards, as far as I know and I cannae fight the Chisolms alone."

Kestar added, "Gilbert, much has happened to them, and the priorities for now should be healing and mourning. We can make plans another day, but for now, we are anxious for a warm bed for the night, if ye'd be so kind."

Finn said, "I can sleep in the stables. I'm accustomed to sleeping there."

"We have plenty of room for ye inside, Finn. Yer horses will be well taken care of, and I'll make sure they are kept hidden so no one will suspect ye are here. In fact, on the morrow we can speak about a place ye can live, if ye like. I have an empty castle that will go to ruin if no one inhabits it. It hasn't been lived in for a while, I'm afraid, but I have been seriously considering renting it to someone. It pains me to see it go to ruin. I would be pleased to see it rented to a good family if ye promise to take fine care of the keep. Something for ye to consider in the next few days. Until then, ye are welcome to stay as long as ye like. All of ye. 'Tis my honor to welcome Ronan's family."

Symon couldn't hide his relief. "I would be happy to discuss that possibility in the next few days. Even to take back our own MacKinnon

Castle will require much work. The walls are crumbled, the furniture destroyed. The marauders set fire to the huts. It will take many hands and much coin to rebuild, but we must first rid the land of the Chisolms. I dinnae know if that is possible." He leaned forward with his elbows resting on his knees. "Mayhap we should consider relocating, starting fresh. 'Tis something for us to think on. I will consider yer offer. But I dinnae know if we have any surviving clan mates yet. There is still much to learn." He took one look at his sister and stood. "If ye dinnae mind, I think we could all use a good night's rest. I cannae thank ye enough for yer hospitality, Gilbert."

Gilbert stood and waved his hand to Symon. "'Tis much to consider, but we can discuss the details another time. Ye must be exhausted from all ye've been through. For now, my maid will show ye to yer chambers, and ye are welcome to stay here for as long as ye need. I have a strong group of guards to keep any strangers at bay. Mabel, please put Alicia in the chamber with the warmest hearth. Kestar can stay in the far chamber."

Symon offered, "Finn can sleep in my chamber if that will help, my lord."

Gilbert let out a deep sigh. "I have more than enough chambers, though I can put the two of ye in a chamber of six beds on the third floor if ye'd prefer."

"That suits me fine."

Finn nodded, and Symon ruffled the red mop of hair in desperate need of a wash.

"Och, and I'll have a tub sent up and filled for Alicia. Mabel will assist ye, my dear. And I'll send hot water for the tub in yer chamber, Symon. There's wood for the hearth if ye dinnae mind caring for it yerself."

"Many thanks to ye. We are exhausted as it was a journey that was rushed. We feared the Chisolms every time we glanced over our shoulder. I am in your debt, my lord."

Gilbert chuckled. "Och, 'tis possible ye are about to become a Highlander. 'Tis yer first lesson that Highlanders must always welcome guests, no matter the reason. We live in cold country for most of the year, and 'tis important that we can depend on each other if a storm is upon us."

"Duly noted," he replied with a chuckle. "And much appreciated. I'll give it some serious thought."

"Have ye sent a messenger to our king? He needs to know of the heinous crime the Chisolms have committed. Shall we consider doing so on the morrow?"

Symon let out a deep sigh. "Eventually, I will be able to face writing such a message. I know it must be done. It willnae bring my family back. But for now, I'm ready to rest my head. The last night we had was comfortable, but the night before, the lad and I spent in the dungeon. Since then we've been on the run, all three of us with our own wounds to heal. Until another day, if ye dinnae mind."

"Understood. Ye willnae find any neighbors of that ilk around here. Of course, we have some

Englishmen no' far who dinnae know anything about being kind to their neighbors, but the morrow is soon enough to learn about them. Welcome to the Highlands, all of ye."

As they headed up the staircase behind Mabel, Symon followed Alicia into her chamber then turned to Finn. "Why do ye no' help bring buckets of warm water for my sister?"

"Aye, my pleasure, Chief." The boy disappeared before Mabel could tell him where to go. Fortunately, Finn was an industrious worker, so Symon was sure he'd find the right place.

"Alicia, ye are fine with Mabel helping ye to undress?" He didn't want to leave his sister alone, but he was equally sure she didn't wish for his help getting into the tub.

"I'll be fine. Mabel, go ahead and show them their chamber first."

Mabel said, "Aye, my lady." They left and Mabel took him down to the end of the passageway. "The staircase is on either end of the floor and the chamber fills the third floor. And you have a clear view of anyone arriving here from the vantage point on this end. If ye are needing anything, just pull on that bell. I'll hear it."

"We'll be fine, Mabel. Please take good care of my sister. She's had a most difficult journey."

Mabel nodded and left.

He climbed the staircase after finding a candle to light the way. Once upstairs he lit the chamber up, pleased to find it was in fine shape, no heavy dust visible and three of the beds had fresh linens on them. Having settled his things, he looked about for the spot Mabel mentioned. Seeing the shutter at the end of the chamber, he opened it and peered out into the night.

The view stunned him, even as night approached. Mountains in the distance, hills everywhere, though because of the darkness it was difficult to see anything clearly besides the mountains. But the nearly full moon lit up the view enough for him to realize they had come to beautiful country indeed.

Closing the shutter, he put some wood in the hearth and lit it, then sat down to remove his boots. He leaned back and rested his head on the chair, surprised that the first thing he saw when he closed his eyes was a pair of blue eyes in a rage, but not directed at him.

Johanna.

The door to the chamber burst open and Finn flew in, spewing words Symon couldn't understand. "Calm down, Finn. Take a deep breath and talk slowly so I can understand ye."

He swallowed hard and pointed. "Horses coming."

Symon didn't need any other explanation. He hurried over to the small window, pulled back the shutters and looked toward the path. Gilbert Morrigan was making his way over to the stables but was approached by three horsemen directly beneath their window. They came from nowhere.

"Who are ye?" Gilbert demanded.

Symon knew and Finn nearly shouted, but Symon clasped his hand over the lad's mouth and pulled him back from the window. "Hush." He put out the candle in the closest sconce to hide their presence. "Listen."

"Clan Chisolm looking for a man named Kestar. We were told he is a friend of yers. He's a healer."

Ten men came out of the stables and another building, bearing swords, their hands at the ready as they gathered behind Gilbert. Symon had to breathe a sigh of relief. He had wondered if the guards would be skilled if trained for a manor home, but he didn't know the way of Highlanders. He hadn't been sure Gilbert would have enough guards, so that much pleased him.

"Kestar is a friend, but he doesnae live here. He lives in the Lowlands. I dinnae recognize yer clan. How far away are ye from yer home?"

"Chisolms have much land in the Lowlands. Enough that we travel freely. Ye need no' worry about why we are here. But Kestar has something that belongs to us and we want it back."

"Ye've wasted a trip into the Highlands. Kestar is no' here. Take yer leave or I'll send for the sheriff. He's no' far."

"We noticed tracks leading here. Have ye any recent visitors?" Symon recognized Malcolm in the front of two other men. He thought one could be Tavish, but the other was definitely not Ewart or their sire.

"Nay, no visitors. My men returned from Dunkeld with foodstuffs. Take yer leave now. I dinnae like being brought out of my home late at night by men I dinnae know." Gilbert whistled and a line of horses came out of the stables, his guards mounting them as orderly as anything Symon had ever seen. "Escort these men off our land."

Tavish said, "No need. We'll be leaving. If ye see Kestar, tell him I want it back."

Symon didn't remove his hand from Finn's mouth until he was sure the lad would not shout and give their presence away.

"'Twas the Chisolms! They followed us." Finn's eyes had widened enough to be painful, Symon thought. He gripped Symon's shoulder hard as he pushed himself away from him. "What does Kestar have that they want? I dinnae understand."

"I do. They want Alicia."

Finn whispered, "Nay. Symon, we must protect yer sister!"

"Promise me ye'll no' tell her what ye heard. They willnae go away easily. I hope they are off searching in another direction, but they want me, Alicia, and our treasures."

"Do ye have any more treasures for them to find?"

Symon smiled and shrugged. "Mayhap."

CHAPTER SIX

SYMON DID NOT sleep well, his dreams bouncing back and forth between an ill-treated dark-haired beauty and his sister Alicia.

In between he had nightmares of Chisolms on horseback, but in his dream, they were on MacKinnon land, killing everyone in sight. He saw so many of his clan mates struck down that when he awakened, he had to push himself to an upright position and walk. Finn was sound asleep so he pulled out the small cask from his sack, removed the top and took a swig of the golden liquid. He swilled it around his mouth, loving the burn of the amber whisky his grandfather had perfected.

He shouldn't have had so much to drink the night of the raid; he couldn't bear to believe he'd been the one to let the Chisolms in. Having searched his memory every day since the day they'd taken over, he had yet to come up with any memory of what the bastard had blamed on him.

He'd had a few black outs when he was younger

from too much whisky and ale, but he'd calmed down. Hadn't he?

Back he went to the shuttered window, opening it to look out over the Highland countryside. He would make it his business to learn the land here, his neighbors, and make sure he met the local sheriff. Somehow, he'd have to build his own group of guards in order to go back and reclaim his clan's heritage. He couldn't let the Chisolms win. His father would want him to return and fight for his land.

He ran his hand down his face, the memories of all he'd seen still fresh. The sections of the curtain wall destroyed by battering rams, the fire burning the huts that so many of their people lived in, the furniture torn apart in the search of treasures. Even their keep, which had been built of timber, had one wall with a gaping hole in it.

He had to wonder if the effort would be worth it. Had the Chisolms finished their attack and destroyed everything or were they rebuilding?

It didn't matter. His sire would want the land to remain in MacKinnon hands.

Much as he wished to return, it was too soon. He wished to send a missive to the king advising him of Chisolm's crimes against his clan. While he knew Alexander didn't wish to be bothered by news of petty clan feuds, this was far worse.

But had Fagan Chisolm already gone to the king with his lies?

Perhaps he should seriously consider Gilbert's offer. If he chose to rent his old place, help him repair and rebuild the abandoned castle, they would have a private place to stay while they considered their options. He could stay for a moon, train new guardsmen, see if any MacKinnon guards traveled this far or if there were new ones to hire. A castle in the Highlands would give him something to do instead of spending all his time hating and planning revenge.

He needed to give Alicia the time to heal. Staying in the Highlands for a short time might be exactly the right thing to do.

If he chose to stay, he would need many to help. And he had to admit, if he managed to find a good number of people willing to work inside Morrigan Castle, perhaps he could consider moving Clan MacKinnon to the Highlands.

First, he needed to see the shape of the castle, see how many could live there. Any huts? What shape were the kitchens in? If it was in good shape, just neglected, then perhaps he could help return it to fine shape.

It would be a major undertaking, but the thought oddly invigorated him. Names of all the trades he'd need to bring the new clan to fruition rolled through his mind. A cook, maids, blacksmith, stablemaster, guards, armorer, brewer, tanner, tailor, so many others. He needed men who could hunt, carpenters who could build huts for his people.

How had his sire done all of that on his own?

One step at a time. Something his sire had often said to his mother, who always worried about everything.

And most of all he needed clansmen and women. Alicia needed companionship. She deserved to have friends. Could it be possible that others survived besides Finn and Alicia? He prayed so.

For now, there was too much to do. He would think about reclaiming his castle in a moon or two but not before then. He owed that to Alicia and Finn. A sharp pain in his thigh reminded him that he needed to heal as well. Lifting his sword could prove to be a bit more difficult than usual.

As soon as he vowed to forget about Malcolm Chisolm and his family, their cruelty resurfaced to remind him that the Chisolms were still looking for them and above all, he needed to consider where they would be safe enough to heal.

Ultimately, he feared they'd never be safe until the Chisolms were dead.

All of them.

He wandered back to his bed, his hand massaging the ache in his leg before he settled down to sleep again, but it was far from restful. However, he was no longer seeing the Chisolms, a small fact he was grateful for.

When he finally awakened, he glanced over at Finn, who was snoring lightly with all the covers thrown off him. The chamber was chilled, but he saw no reason to light a fire, instead he covered Finn, washed up with a basin of water, and then headed down the stairs.

He was anxious to hear if anything else had happened with the Chisolms so he crept down the staircase as quietly as he could, hoping not to awaken anyone. When he finally arrived in the great hall, Kestar and Gilbert were deep in discussion in front of the hearth.

Gilbert said, "Join us, please. We have warm broth for ye and some fresh bread to start. Cook will have more later, but we are up a wee bit early.

Symon said, "Many thanks. I heard ye had visitors last eve. I tried to listen from the window, but I dinnae know if I heard all. They were looking for Kestar, not me?"

"'Tis what he said. Said Tavish wanted what Kestar took." Gilbert peered at his friend. Symon had to admit that Kestar was looking a bit haggard this morn.

Kestar sighed and tugged on his long beard. "I have naught of his. The only thing he gave me was a person, yer sister. She doesnae belong to him, so I'm no' sure what the daft man meant by that statement."

"I would wager that now that they no longer have me and still havenae found our treasure, he's wishing he'd kept Alicia in the hopes that hurting her would make me give up the treasure they think I have." Symon rubbed his throbbing leg, glad he had a reminder of the cruelty of the bastards.

Gilbert said, "I know this is wrong, but it must be stated. If ye truly have a treasure of some sort, Symon, would it no' benefit ye to give them what they wish so ye'll be free of them?"

"Impossible," replied Symon. "True, I've knowledge of the location of a few gemstones but if I gave it to them, Fagan would still no' be happy. He wants the barrels of whisky my grandsire made over the years."

"Then why not give them to him?" Gilbert asked.

Kestar added, "'Twould do ye good to give up the drink of the golden liquid, Symon."

"Ye think ye know why, but ye dinnae. I gave my grandsire my word that I would protect his creation with my life. I can do no less with it. I know where most of it is but there are casks in different locations. He was nearly daft trying to save it for our clan. It was his recipe that he worked on for years. Grandsire carried a great deal of pride in making those barrels of golden liquid. I cannae just hand them over to Fagan. My grandsire would rise from his grave if I did."

Gilbert said, "Give him one or two barrels. He'll no' be able to drink it in his lifetime."

Symon would not budge on this matter, but Gilbert apparently couldn't understand what it meant for him to have given his word to his grandsire. There was no point in continuing this conversation about what else he should hand over to the Chisolms. They'd taken enough already.

They'd taken his family, killed many of his clan, destroyed his home, but more importantly, his pride. He had to regain something, and at the moment, pride was the only choice.

"I'd like to discuss something else, if ye please. Please tell me more about your castle. I've come to realize that our safety is paramount, and to guarantee that my dearest sister is not harmed again that we may need to stay in the Highlands for at least a moon or so. I would be glad to assist ye in repairing and rebuilding yer castle in return for our living there for a wee bit. I have some rent I can pay, but I'd like to work off some of the cost if possible."

Gilbert wandered over to the hearth and stared into the fire for a few moments before he took a chair a distance away from the flames, indicating for the other two to sit down. "'Tis my clan's land and was my home before the worst day of my life. The day my dear wife gave birth was the happiest day of our lives. Unfortunately, she became weaker and weaker every day after then. I was able to watch the two together, enjoying the delight the wee lass gave to both of us is my favorite memory of all. We lost my dear wife Elspeth about a sennight later. The nanny found wet nurses for wee Moira, something I was incapable of doing because I was beside myself with grief. How could the Lord take my dear wife away after giving us such a gift? I'll never know the answer to that question.

"The worst day grew into something even more painful as the days passed. Apparently, the healers who came to assist us because Kestar was away did no' pay close enough attention to the new bairn. She only lived several days after Elspeth and died in her cradle. I was told that she was found dead one morn and the wet nurse removed the bairn and took it to the kirk to be blessed. They tried everything but my sweet lass died. My wife wished to name her after her mother. Moira Morrigan was to be her name, but it was no' to be."

"My deepest sympathy for such a heavy loss. She wasnae born here?"

"Nay, in the keep of the castle that neighbors here. After we lost my wife and wee lassie, word carried that I was cursed. Once that word traveled among my people, they began to leave slowly. Part of it was because I was so grief-stricken that I no longer took care of my clan's needs. And Elspeth was not here to help me either. I forgot to order supplies, we ran out of oats for the horses. The Cook complained she needed more vegetables, more grains, but I ignored her. She left for a neighboring clan. I think my clan's people hoped something would give me a jolt back to taking care of our castle, but nothing did.

"Then we had a fire in one of the upstairs chambers, filling the keep with so much smoke that it was nearly unlivable. Even more left then. No cook, a smoke-filled keep, a great hall that was a mess. It was only a matter of time, and I am to blame for it all. I accept the responsibility, but I didnae care.

"No one has attempted to live there because of the fire. Between the gossip of the curse upon my clan and the fire, something that fueled the curse even more, many more left to find other places to live. I heard some built their own small village about an hour north of here. But again, it falls on my shoulders. I didnae care and couldnae bear to live there with so many memories, so I moved here.

"I'll take ye there once the sun is up and ye may decide but say naught until ye see it. The fire was in one of the bedchambers above stairs, but it left a hole in the roof so critters have moved in. 'Tis much to do to make it livable, but I can loan ye a dozen of my guards to assist ye. They do little but protect, though some have other skills that could benefit ye. But they would be on loan. I'd like to keep them as guards here." He glanced from Kestar then back to Symon. "What say ye? Will ye help me rebuild my neglected castle? I'll allow ye to live there until ye are ready to go south as long as ye help me fix what needs to be repaired."

"I am able to pay some rent, but I'd be pleased and honored to help ye rebuild. It will give me a sense of purpose and force me to allow Alicia to heal."

Kestar chuckled. "Ye worry about yer sister verra much, but ye also need time to heal, Symon. And ye both need time to grieve for all ye've lost. Ye will not be any good to anyone until ye do both a wee bit. But aye, safety for all three of ye is first."

"I'd be deeply indebted to ye, my lord, if we can live there for rent or trade. Probably best for us to move away before our presence causes more trouble for ye."

Gilbert snorted. "I'm no' afraid of a Lowland chieftain. Yer sire taught me much about chieftains and the Lowlands. In fact, I nearly had him convinced once to come to the Highlands and start over. He mentioned being frustrated with his neighbors, but never a word on which one. Mayhap he disliked the Chisolms all along. Enough talk for now. Break yer fast and let me know when ye are ready to travel. I dinnae doubt the Chisolms will return in the daylight either this day or the morrow. But we shall wait as I'm assuming ye'd like Finn and Alicia to come along."

"Aye, I would."

"Where are we going?" Alicia asked from the top of the staircase, making her way gracefully down and heading toward them. "Please dinnae say we are returning to Clan MacKinnon yet. I cannae go with ye if so, Symon."

Gilbert smiled and answered, "To see yer new home possibly."

"We hope," Kestar added.

Gilbert said, "I'm going out to the stables to speak to my guards. Enjoy yer food and I'll return soon."

Once he was gone, Symon helped Alicia settle in a comfortable chair and brought her a goblet of warm broth. "I wish to discuss this with ye, sister."

"I'm ready. For ye to talk, no' to return home."

"How are ye feeling?"

"Much better. I have little pain," she replied, playing with her goblet.

Symon could tell she was lying, but he was unsure how to interpret the lie. Was it physical pain or emotional? Was she reliving her attack as he had several times already? Or was she so sore it pained her to walk? "I think Gilbert and I have come to an arrangement, but I would like yer opinion. Based on what ye have shared already, I think we have made the right decision, but I wish for yer approval."

"Go ahead, Symon. Whatever we choose willnae be easy, but I must insist that we stay together. I couldnae bear to lose ye at this point."

"Nor I ye," he whispered. "Gilbert's castle has been neglected ever since he moved here. He was hoping to hire me to help repair the castle, clean up whatever is necessary, and to hire and train more guards. At least that is one of my goals. He left about a year after his wife and daughter passed on and has never returned. There was a fire at that time, and many of his people left because they believed the castle or Gilbert were cursed."

"'Tis silly but go on. What would ye like to do?" She took a sip of her broth and sighed with pleasure. She said, "'Tis the most simplest pleasures in life I choose to appreciate from now on. A good broth in the morn is one."

"Agreed. Gilbert has offered us the castle to clean and to stay in until we are ready to return to Clan MacKinnon. I'd like to hear from ye how long ye think that will be."

She nearly bolted from her chair, but she refrained. "Never. I dinnae wish to go back there when Malcolm and Tavish and Ewart are all looking for me or ye. There is naught left for us. Ye said all our people are gone. We should rebuild here and start a new Clan MacKinnon just as Great-Grandsire did so many years ago."

"So ye would like to stay in Gilbert's castle, Morrigan Castle?"

"Aye, once we see if we can make it livable again. I will work with ye, brother. But I dinnae wish to go back to the Lowlands." She stared into his eyes, and Symon was surprised to see how serious she was about that declaration. That did take him by surprise.

"Ye know that when I have the men to return with me, I will go back to see the situation, or to try to regain our land."

"Go ahead and look, but I'll not be returning. I dinnae wish to be anywhere near the Chisolms. Besides, ye told me it was all destroyed. Why would ye go back if there was naught there? Did ye no' say that even the furniture was destroyed? Part of the keep? The curtain wall? The beds? Why return?"

Symon rubbed his hands together while he considered her answer. She had the right of it in many ways. "Curiosity. Male pride. Because I believe Da would want me to return. I'm not sure what reason exactly, but I feel compelled to go back. But not yet."

Her eyes misted quickly, something that did take him by surprise. "Please no' for at least two moons, Symon, and dinnae ask me to go with ye. Promise me."

"I'll never press ye to return. 'Tis yer choice, lass. I'm no' sure if I'll wait two moons, but I can promise one. Will that please ye?"

She swiped her tears from her cheeks. "Aye, for now. I cannae say how I'll feel in a moon, but as long as I know ye'll be by my side for that long, I will sleep better."

He reached over and clasped one of her hands in his. "I will promise that much. Will ye go with us to see the castle?"

"Aye. I would love to. Once I get something to eat. I am hungry this morn."

Finn came barreling down the stairs behind her. "Is there food left? Am I too late to break my fast?"

Just then, the cook came into the hall with a large pot of oats. "Nay, ye are just in time. Lots of porridge and I'll get the honey and berries ye may add if ye like."

Nearly two hours later, they crested a ridge and Symon stopped his horse, Alicia stopping next to him. "Are ye all right, Symon? Is something wrong?" The others had stopped also simply because he had.

"Naught is wrong. I'm admiring the view. I had no idea this castle was as large as it is. 'Tis beautiful and clearly once a wonderful castle. And a lovely loch not far away." He pointed off to one side of the castle where a small loch sat, the entire place looking quite majestic in the middle of a spring meadow.

"Och, but much is in disrepair. Keep an open mind when we step inside the keep." Gilbert took the lead, taking them through the open gate, into the cobblestone courtyard and over to the steps leading up to the keep. Before they dismounted, he pointed out a few points of interest. "A creek runs from the back of the loch and behind the castle wall. We used it for water, I never saw it run dry. There is a lovely waterfall not far from here. The wall, as ye can see, is damaged over there. It will need repairing as the stone has crumbled. You'll need to take a hard look at the entire curtain wall to see if it has deteriorated in other spots. The rest looks the same, though you can see we had no shutters on the windows, just thick furs to keep the cold at bay. They've fallen off, a way for the wildlife to get in, birds, mice, whatever."

"Is there a cellar?" Symon asked.

"Aye, a fine area for storage, the buttery, though I've taken all the buttes of ale. Took all the grain sacks too, though I don't think the mice approved of that. A few cells for the worst among us, though Elspeth hated the idea that there was a dungeon beneath her feet. We never called it such. Come, we'll go inside and ye can see fer yerself. The kitchens are attached to the back by a covered walkway."

They left their horses near a grassy area surrounding the center of the courtyard. "Looks like this was a garden at some point," Alicia said, studying the plants in the area. "I see some nice spices here."

"Elspeth loved spicing up supper meals. She took great pride in her garden, though I cannae tell ye what she planted."

They moved up the steps and Gilbert held the door to the keep open, allowing Symon and Finn to step inside first, Alicia behind them.

Inside, they took another set of four steps up to the left that led to the great hall. Symon stepped inside and moved to the middle of the hall, letting out a low whistle. "'Tis most lovely. A fine hall with a beautiful hearth at each end. The floor is solid and you have many trestle tables. No one took them?"

"Nay, we had plenty. You'll find stools in the kitchens and in the basement. We did take the large armed chairs that sat in front of the hearth on the left, my favorite chairs. The beds should still be there except for the back bedchamber where the fire was. We took the linens, pillows, and furs, of course. But ye'll find empty chests and some chairs too. Ye won't be in need of much furniture, just mattresses, linens, and cushions."

As they spoke, a mouse ran across the floor with a high-pitched squeak, as if to tell the invaders to leave. Finn ran above stairs while Alicia moved toward the kitchens. "I'll go with ye, sister. Finn can check the bedchambers."

The kitchens were large, many pots still there, a good deal of workspace and some spices still hanging from the ceiling. Alicia said, "This is twice the size of our kitchens, Symon. We could make this into a large clan. Do ye think any of our clan mates have survived besides us?"

"Possibly, but there is no way for me to reach out to them until Fagan Chisolm changes his mind about coming after us. But we can welcome any of the locals looking for a new home, especially once we've built up the guards so we can offer protection. Gilbert said that some of his clan rebuilt a village not far. Perhaps they would consider returning. Obviously some stayed with him, but many considered him cursed and left to go out on their own." He glanced at every wall, at the solid rafters, and just at the general size of the place. "We may find more than we expected. Once we have moved in, adjusted, we can ask more questions about a cook and carpenters. I noticed five small cottages in the back inside the curtain wall. Their roofs are in need of repair, but that can be done with a few strong men.

"But first we must decide if this is to be our new home for now. Alicia, would ye feel safe here if we found several guards to work with us?" He had to ask the question because he wouldn't risk losing his sister, yet he didn't wish to live without her either. They had memories, many of them sweet.

"Aye, but what do ye think, Symon? Can we handle it? There is much to be done in a short time to make it livable."

His gaze searched the area before he nodded his answer. "I think we can. I'll go to market, look for some men looking for a place to live. Or mayhap Gilbert knows of men who left him who would return willingly to the castle. 'Tis possible. And it would get our minds off all that has transpired of late."

"I believe ye are correct." Just then Finn popped through the doorway. "There are five large bedchambers on the second floor, only one destroyed by the fire. But that area is enclosed so we cannot use it. The damage is inside the bedchamber, clear as ash from the hearth. I think there are another two chambers on the third floor."

"Ye did no' investigate?"

"Nay. That staircase is made of wood and is falling apart in one spot. I didnae trust it." Finn gave him a small grin. "Shall we move in, Symon? We could make this verra comfortable, I think. We just need more men to help us."

Alicia said, "We need to come up with our list of needs and head back to Dunkeld to the market. 'Twill take us all day to find what we need. Bedcoverings, furs, foodstuffs. Soaps, scented candles, brooms. We have much to do, but I look forward to it, Symon." She hesitated then peered up at her brother again. "We need something to take our mind from all that has transpired. And if Gilbert will lend us his guards for a few days, we should be able to ready this place to be livable and have some protection until we find our own guards. Do we have the coin to do what we need to do?"

"Aye, I grabbed a bag that Ewart was holding when I left. There's enough coin to get us a good start."

"Then aye, I think we can make this into a fine clan. To hell with the Chisolms."

"That's my feisty sister. We'll make a go of it. We'll tell Gilbert and get started right away."

There was only one issue that still churned in his gut. Malcolm Chisolm coming for his sister. He wouldn't risk her life or Finn's. Perhaps they could live with Gilbert until more guards could be found and trained.

But then he thought of her in a different place, something he didn't want. He adored his sister and wished to live with her. He'd just have to find the guards to protect her.

He was certain of one thing. If any Chisolm came near her, he would kill them without thinking twice about it. To make sure she would be safe, he would have to begin working his sword skills again soon. No matter how much it hurt.

He wanted a sip of whisky.

CHAPTER SEVEN

T HE GROUP OF ten, Symon, Alicia, and Finn along with seven guards, headed to Dunkeld by mid-afternoon. Symon insisted they remove their plaids and dressed in plain clothing so they wouldn't be quickly identifiable by the Chisolms, just in case they crossed paths.

Alicia had been quite concerned. "Are ye sure Ewart willnae be looking for us? For me?"

"We'll take guards with us, and we all must find different clothes. I'll no' wear the MacKinnon plaid at all until this is over. Will that make ye feel better?"

"Aye, but we must move quickly. Please, Symon. Dinnae make yerself obvious."

"We know what we want so it shouldnae take long. I doubt they are looking for us in the middle of the market. They are probably going from castle to castle, just as they did the other night. Gilbert said his wife was about yer size and gave me this gown for ye."

It was a plain brown wool gown, nothing that would make her stand out, but he knew Alicia liked to look pretty. Would this work or not?

"What do ye think? Will ye wear it?" He held it out for her and her eyes widened.

"Aye, 'tis perfect. Please tell Gilbert I appreciate this verra much."

Neither one of them had any extra clothing with them, so they would be forced to shop for fabric. By the time they dressed and readied the group near the stable, Symon believed they were totally unrecognizable.

Once they arrived, Symon decided his sister would have the best judgment for this excursion. "Alicia, where shall we go first?"

"Gilbert said there is a large shop that carries nearly everything. I think he said it was on High Street."

"But we need to go to the tailor and the tanner, the glover…"

"Aye, Symon. But we need cleaning supplies and makings for the beds first. We'll get the basics first. We have time to come back for the gloves and boots. Though I could use a new gown. I do appreciate that Gilbert gave me this one his wife wore, but 'tis verra itchy for me."

"We'll see what they have inside this shop. See what the merchant recommends as to where to purchase our other supplies." Symon's hand was on Finn's shoulder, keeping him close because the lad's gaze wandered everywhere. "We'll find some yer size also, Finn."

Finn didn't even hear him, he was too busy watching whatever was happening in the center of the town. "Can I no' stay out here a wee bit longer?"

"Aye," Symon replied. "Until ye're needed to carry supplies out to the cart."

He nodded excitedly and said, "I promise not to wander. I'll stay right here."

Symon stepped inside the shop with Alicia, allowing his gaze to adjust to the change in light. The shop was large, and there were people milling about looking at goods, so Symon said, "I'd say start in the back corner. I believe I see linens back there."

Alicia said, "Have we enough coin for some or all? Finn could sleep in the stables."

"We dinnae have a stable yet. I hope we will soon. We'll need to find some straw before that can happen. Aye, I have Da's coins, so we have more than enough. And I have a couple of jewels from Da's sword if necessary, though please tell no one. We do no' need them yet. Purchase what we need to clean the keep so it no longer smells. We need brooms and shovels, but ye need cleaning supplies, whatever it takes to make the smell better. Rushes? Lavender from the rafters? Whatever ye need, lass. I wish we had someone to help ye, but we dinnae yet. Buy linens for half a dozen beds. And furs for the windows and blankets. Some pillows."

She piled all she needed on one empty table at the periphery. The owner of the shop saw the amount they were purchasing and joined them quickly. "Have ye need for anything else? Foodstuffs? Clothing?"

"Aye. Have ye any gowns already made?"

"Nay, the tailor down the street can help ye,

but I do have a night rail about yer size and some tunics for yer husband. I have oats and sugar, barley, some salt. I even have a bag of freshly picked vegetables brought in trade earlier today. Would ye be interested?"

"Aye, we'll take the foodstuffs and the vegetables." Alicia glanced up at Symon, who made no attempt to correct the man behind the table. It was fine with her if word got around that they were a married couple. Perhaps they'd be left alone. "I need some extra linen fabric. And some buckets."

The man moved on to help with Alicia's choices, piling them all on the table. When they were finished, they whistled for Finn to help, then left their purchases in the cart they'd brought and moved toward the tailor. Symon said, "Go on inside and see if he has anything ye can use yet. If no', we'll come back another day to make an order. The sun is dropping quickly, and I wish to buy bread and a butte of ale along with some meat pies before we leave." Finn moved to a spot where he could see the center of the courtyard.

"All right, ye go ahead and I'll meet ye back here in a quarter hour, Symon. Tell Finn to watch our cart."

"The packages are hidden under a large woolen blanket."

"Still, we cannae lose any of it."

"Understood." Symon searched for Finn after he purchased his items, surprised to see him now running straight toward him.

"Symon, ye'll no' like this." He stopped because

he was so out of breath from running, but he pointed off to a platform in the middle of the street. There was a small crowd gathering around the platform. "The lad. They're about to cut off his hand, said he was a thief but his sire swears he did no' steal anything."

More bullies.

He strode over, listening to all the comments, the poor lad sobbing, his father was begging the man in the middle who apparently was the accuser. It was easy to determine who the bully was just by his words. "'Tis my right to see that justice is served."

"But there are others who say it was a different lad, not my son. Master Smalley, Davie didnae do this." The man had dark hair, kept shorter than Symon's, but he was doing all he could to save his son.

The man tied the boy's hand to the trunk of a tree, then pulled out a large axe, sharpening the edges. "I'll do ye a favor and sharpen this so it will cut it off clean. Others have had to strike the bone three times to cut through all the way."

The lad turned his head and heaved on the ground.

The man jumped back and said, "Do not dare to heave your insides all over me, or I'll cut your other hand off too."

The man looked familiar to him, but he couldn't place him. Then he recalled. He was one of the men who had been with Johanna. Cruel with a twisted sense of right and wrong. A bully to women and lads.

He couldn't let it happen.

"I'll take the lad under my wing. No need to perform such a ludicrous action. I'll be responsible for him."

"Not until justice is served." Smalley stalked off, saying, "I'll return momentarily. I must sharpen this blade."

The boy's father turned around and said, "My thanks to ye, but he's my son. I'll no' give him up."

Symon said, "Where do ye live?"

"We live with the Smalleys but he's never liked my son."

"What is yer work at the Smalleys?"

"I'm the stablemaster and my son assists. My wife is the cook, and our daughter helps in the kitchens."

"I am Symon MacKinnon, Chieftain of Clan MacKinnon. I'm in need of a cook and a stablemaster. I can pay ye a fair wage or give ye a place to live in return for yer loyalty."

"If ye can save my son, we will come with ye." The expression on the man's face was one of desperation.

"Fair enough. We're about to leave. Come with us now." Symon reached over and untied the lad's hand. "Ye are coming with me, Davie, and ye'll need both hands."

The boy's face lit up as he wiggled his hand once it was freed. A voice came from behind him. "You there. The lad will stay for his punishment. He stole an apple from the barrel in the stables. Actually ate it himself." He raced over and said, "I'll not have all our help stealing from Henry

Smalley. I must set an example." The man's beady eyes looked as though he would enjoy cutting off the boy's hand.

"I solved yer problem. He's no longer yer help, he's mine." He tucked the lad inside him to protect him in case Henry Smalley began to swing the axe about him.

Finn grabbed the father's hand shouting, "This way. Our cart is here. I'll ride with Alicia and ye can have my horse."

When they approached the cart, Alicia came out of the tailor shop with a package, looking strangely at Symon, but he just shrugged his shoulders. "We have a new stablemaster, but we must hurry, Alicia."

"I'm finished. I found one I can adjust so I'm pleased." She tossed the package in the cart and Symon lifted her onto the horse. "What's yer name?" Alicia asked, looking over Symon's shoulder at the bellowing man coming toward her. When she noticed the chaos growing behind her, she said, "I think we should hurry. I'll find out later."

"Liam, and this is Davie.

They mounted and looked to Symon who said, "North. We're heading north."

They made it away from the crowds, though the cart was nearly tipping over. They had to hurry. "Can we go get my wife now?"

"I think we should, or he'll be cutting yer daughter's hand off next. Lead the way." Symon wouldn't take any chances with Henry Smalley.

Their horses moved through the crowds easily, probably because they were large beasts and many were afraid of them, especially Nightmare. Either way, half the hour later and they were nearly at Smalley's when Liam stopped his horse so he could speak with Symon. "Many thanks to ye, but I think I must sneak in the back to get my wife. There's a back path that will head north once I find her. And our cottage is over there. Davie, run and pack some clothing for each of us. Whatever ye can."

Finn said, "I'll go along and help."

"While ye are doing that, I'll tie some of the packages to the horses. I fear we may have to leave quickly and I dinnae wish to lose our purchases. The only thing I can't tie on is the oats." Symon looked around but then said, "Hell, I'll just carry them."

The lads returned about the same time as the man with his wife and daughter. "My wife Maud and daughter Meggy.

Alicia said, "The lass can ride with me."

Liam said, "Davie, ride with Finn and Maud will ride with me."

They fussed with the sacks and packages, rearranging everything. They were about to leave when Symon felt someone staring at him.

He turned around, surprised to see Johanna standing there. More beautiful than he remembered, she asked, "Maud, ye are leaving us?"

"Aye, Johanna, I must. I cannae allow that beast

to cut my son's hand off." She reached for her son's hand and kissed it before mounting the horse with her husband's assistance.

"I will miss ye," Johanna mumbled.

"Say naught, Johanna," Symon said. "If ye'd like to come with us, just say so. We are building a new clan."

Her eyes widened and she took a step back as if appalled by the idea.

Symon said, "If ye ever change yer mind, get word to the MacKinnon and I will come for ye."

He left, with a wave of his hand.

An ache in his heart told him he was making a big mistake leaving Johanna there with the Smalleys.

But he'd offered.

And she'd declined.

CHAPTER EIGHT

JOHANNA WATCHED THE group leave with an ache in her heart. A small part of her wished to yell out, "Stop! I'll go with you."

But it made no sense. She'd heard that Henry was taking Davie to Dunkeld to stand his punishment in front of a crowd, something Henry loved to do. He appeared to get a twisted pleasure from hurting others. But Davie was now with the huge Highlander who had helped her up when she'd fallen to the ground.

The man had more honor in his little finger than Henry Smalley possessed in his entire body. And he was even more handsome this day than he'd been the day before.

In fact, if she were honest, she'd admit that the man nearly set her heart a fluttering.

Nearly.

She closed the door to the curtain wall and grabbed a bucket near the well, managing to fill it up so she wouldn't look like she was involved in Cook's escape. The sisters were equally cruel to the wee lass Meggy, so she was actually happy for the two. Maud and Meggy deserved happiness.

She recalled the time Aldreda had been unhappy with the stew Maud served for supper one eve. She'd picked up her bowl and threw it at the wall, stew flying everywhere. "This is disgusting food. Now clean it up and make something more appealing."

Poor Maud had been shocked, clearly so confused that she had no better food to offer other than bread and a fruit tart. Henry had brought out a bottle of French wine just to quiet his sister with all her complaints.

Aldreda even exhausted her own brother.

She ducked inside the kitchen door, carrying the bucket of water carefully so as not to spill it. After setting it down, she stood letting out a deep sigh. She'd made it without being seen near Maud and Meggy.

A deep voice came from behind her. It was Barnard, Rohesia's husband, Aldreda's brother. "What have you done, Johanna? Where are they?"

So startled she was grateful she hadn't been still holding the bucket or the water would have surely spilled over. "Who are you asking about? I just came from the well." She stood back, wanting to be as far away from Barnard as she could. He made her skin crawl.

"Maud and Meggy. They are gone. Tell me where they are?"

"I…I…know not what you mean. They were here a moment ago. Maud asked me to get water for her to cook with. So I did as she asked. When I returned, there was no one here."

Barnard stepped closer, his eyes narrowing. When he was so close that he could touch her, he reached out and squeezed her breast.

She pushed his hand away, stunned that he would touch her so inappropriately, but she dared not say anything. His fetid breath reached her and she dropped her gaze, hoping that lowering her nose would improve the air about her.

"You dare to push me away?" he whispered.

The door burst open, Henry doing his best to fill the doorway but he was too short, though his belly had widened considerably of late. "Where is she? Someone said that bastard who saved Davie was out back with Liam, collecting Maud and Meggy while they packed their things. Who is that bastard who continues to interfere with our lives?"

He grabbed Johanna and yanked her forward. "Who is he? He likes you so you must know him. Where is he from? I wish to know where he lives. Tell me now!"

Johanna was so frightened that all she could do was shake her head. Henry stood in front of her, babbling in a fury while Barnard was behind her, his hands now stroking her bottom.

"Barnard, you have a wife, do you not?"

"Aye, but I was just touching. She's younger, more pleasing." His sick grin told her Barnard had some odd desires inside him.

"Take your hands from the help. Johanna, you will have one more chance to tell me where that man has taken my stablemaster and my cook. If you don't tell me all you know, you'll spend the night in the basement in our own little dungeon room."

She did her best to calm her fears, though it would be difficult to keep it inside. She hated that room, hated the cellar because the rats lived there.

She hated rats more than anything.

Taking into consideration all she'd seen, there was only one thing she could say. "Aye, they left with him, but I do not know him. I have no idea where he lives or where they were going. Please, I'm telling you the truth."

Henry spat on the floor. "We'll see if you'll tell all after a night with the rats. And don't scream all night because I detest being kept awake. Barnard, you'll stay away from her."

The two men each took an arm and tugged her forward. "Nay, please. I've told you all I know. I have no idea who he is."

Henry opened the door to the cellar and shoved her ahead of him while he grabbed a nearby torch to light the way, He pushed her again when she was nearly at the bottom, forcing her to lose her balance and fall the rest of the way. She landed on her belly on the cold stone floor. She lifted her head and stared straight into the face of a rat scurrying along the perimeter of the cellar.

She should have gone with the strange man. She'd been a fool to reject his offer.

Once they arrived at the castle, they moved inside the gates, then closed the portcullis to outsiders. Symon was surprised to see Gilbert was at the curtain wall where it had crumbled, directing a group of his guards to repair what they could.

Symon called out to the group, "Please come inside when ye can. I have meat pies and bread for all."

They all helped carry the packages inside. Maud and Alicia cleaned off one table and they sat down to eat.

Alicia said, "I'm sure ye are confused and worried, but let me explain a wee bit. I'm Alicia, Symon's sister. We lost our castle in the Lowlands to a vicious attack, so we are relocating here, rebuilding, if ye wish. I promise my brother will treat ye all well. He is Chieftain of Clan MacKinnon, what we hope to build here."

Symon overheard his sister's introduction but decided not to correct her at this point. His plan was to return to MacKinnon land and reclaim what belonged to his ancestors, but now was not the time to argue with her. She had a fear that wasn't anything he could understand as a man. This much he would respect.

Maud finished chewing, then looked around at the hall, asking, "Liam, how did ye meet them and decide to join them?"

Liam explained about how close their son had been to losing his hand and that Symon had saved him. "He is starting anew and offered us a place to stay if we handle the horses here. Maud, Henry threatened to cut off both of his hands because he heaved from fear. I could no' allow that to happen to our boy."

Meggy said, "I hate the Smalleys. They were all so mean. Even the littlest one. Ibb likes to kick everyone and I have bruises as proof."

Maud reached over and pulled Meggy closer. "Ye'll no' have to be subjected to their demands any longer."

Symon sat down after puttering and straightening a few things. "We are pleased to have ye all with us."

"But ye are just acquiring this castle?"

"Aye," Symon said. "This empty castle belongs to Gilbert Morrigan, a friend of our sire. My sister and I lost our parents not long ago, so we are here in the Highlands to start anew. We'd like to make this castle our home and invite many to join us, especially those who left his clan before. 'Tis a long story for another day but understand that we are here to rebuild and repair this castle. 'Twas a gift from Lord Morrigan in exchange for our hard work. He hasn't lived here in many years. He doesn't wish to see it neglected so I said we would be willing to repair what we can. We'd be pleased if ye would join us. We are looking for honest, hard-working people."

Maud said, "My mother was part of Clan Morrigan, but she's been gone for over ten years. My sister would love to join us if ye are looking for more. She and her husband live in a small village with a few others, but she fears attacks. They've seen more and more marauders about. Her family is less than an hour away. I know she'd be thrilled to have the protection of a clan and a curtain wall. She could help me cook or could work as a maid for ye and yer sister," Maud said.

"What is yer sister's name?"

"Elayne. And she is married with two lads and a lass."

Finn said, "Aye, please bring the lads. How many winters? I'd hope for around ten."

Liam smiled. "Well, Davie here is nine and my nephews are six and eight, while my niece is the same as Meggy. They are ten winters, both of them. And their father Andrew is a carpenter."

"We can definitely find work for him if he's interested." Symon couldn't be more pleased. The castle was coming together. Once they finished eating, Alicia took over making the beds ready for the group above stairs.

Symon explained, "There are five huts inside the curtain wall. They need cleaning and probably some repairs, but ye are welcome to one, Liam, and Maud, yer sister's family could have one of the others. But for this night, ye may have one of the large chambers above stairs until the cottage is ready for ye. We havenae checked them so we have no idea which ones are in the best shape. One of the chambers was damaged by fire many years ago. We'll eventually repair it to be used, but no' yet. There are other more pressing needs."

They finished their short meal and went their separate ways, the men cleaning out the heavy dust and critters in the hall while Alicia and Maud set to the bedchambers. The hearths all needed cleaning as did the kitchens, but to clean all was too much for one day. They cleaned out one hearth in the hall and settled three of the bedchambers.

Gilbert came inside, his men following, grabbing an ale and a meat pie. "Many thanks to ye, Symon. I can see ye'll make this castle fine again. We'll spread the word to families we know we can trust, send them yer way, but ye have a stablemaster and I heard talk of a carpenter on his way also. 'Tis true?

"Aye, and I'm pleased there will be two women too. I didnae want Alicia to be the only female here."

Gilbert and his men finished their meal. "We'll head back to my land. I'll gift ye with a goat and a few chickens to get ye started so ye'll have milk and eggs. We'll return on the morrow to finish that spot in the wall. It should keep ye protected. I'll bring some loaves of bread from our cook. Ye can spend the morrow cleaning the kitchens and readying it to prepare food. Mayhap have the lads weed that garden, see what plants have survived. And plant a few more with all the seeds ye told me about."

Maud said, "I'll have some stew started by midday if the men go hunting in the morn. Alicia brought a basket of vegetables and with a couple of rabbits or with luck, a boar, we can eat well. We'll have this place shining soon. And more mouths to feed on their way so I must be prepared."

"I brought sacks of foodstuffs for the pantry,

and I'm glad you saw the large sack of vegetables," Alicia said. "They were freshly picked."

"Perfect for stew and enough to save half for another day."

Once Gilbert left with his men, the lasses returned to the bedchambers sorting basins and placing candles. Symon said to Finn and Davie, "Why do ye lads no' bring water in for the lasses? We'll need some to freshen up on the morrow. They'll find buckets and pitchers for ye."

The lads raced up the staircase, giving Symon the chance to ask the question he needed to ask of Liam. "The woman who came outside at the Smalleys. I believe her name is Johanna. What is her relationship to the Smalleys?"

"Johanna? She was bought from her parents two years ago to service Aldreda and Rohesia as they saw fit. She is nanny to Rohesia's two and maid in general. She's a sweet lass but no' married. Why do ye ask?"

"Because the Smalleys are cruel to her. I saw them treat her poorly in Dunkeld. The poor lass tripped and fell, and they ridiculed her and yelled at her. Even the wee lass kicked her."

"Jocosa kicks everyone, to her father's delight. They are a cruel family, and a tough family to work for. They dinnae appreciate anything ye do for them, and they never pay the coin promised us. We didnae have to pay for our home, but we had to pay for any food that Maud brought home for us. Scraps, leftovers. They charged us for everything. I wish Johanna had come along. I hear she will be betrothed by year's end."

"To whom?" Symon asked, a sudden chill going up his spine. He chastised himself for caring anything about the woman who now had rejected him twice.

"They havenae named him yet, but I'm sure there will be a large payment involved. Not from the bride's family but to the Smalleys. They'll finagle some way to profit from her marriage. I just hope they find a kind man for her."

Symon had an odd feeling in the pit of his belly. As if he knew this would turn out badly. That she'd be betrothed to someone who would not treat her right.

But what could he do about it?

Naught. Absolutely naught.

CHAPTER NINE

JOHANNA SHIVERED AGAINST the stone wall, sitting on the only stool in the chamber. Sounds of scurrying creatures carried to her, and she fought the tears that threatened to break out in a deluge across her face. If one rat came inside her cell, she would scream until she had no voice left. There was a pallet on the floor, but she wouldn't sleep. She had heard tales of men waking up in the middle of the night to find a rat chewing on one of their toes.

Never. Never would that happen to her because she refused to fall asleep.

There were two blankets. She shook them both free of any insects, then chose the better of the two to cover her lap because the cellar was deathly cold. The other one she placed under the door so no rats would sneak underneath.

Footsteps echoed down the staircase. Was it Henry or Barnard?

Henry's face appeared in the window. "Have you come to your senses yet?"

"I do not know anything about that man. How can I come to my senses? He was kind to me in the village, but I don't know anything more than that."

"You better think of something. That foolish bastard is going to ruin everything." Henry began to pace back and forth in the passageway, ignoring her. "How can I take over that castle if I don't get more men? I need more guards, yet Barnard is no help at all. Why can he not learn the skill, become a good leader to advise the men on how to fight, how to protect themselves, how to protect their leader? Me!" He paced and mumbled like a daft person, but Johanna would not interrupt.

"I have too many problems, of course. First, I hear someone has moved into the castle I wish to steal away from Morrigan, the fool. I hate him. But word has it he had visitors and now they are moving in. But someone else said they were just staying a night or two. How can I determine the truth? Should I go there? Go to Gilbert and ask him? Should I just run into the group and ask them? Or shall I just wait until they are gone? Then I could take over myself. And since my cook and stablemaster left, now I must replace them. I have several who would work as a stablemaster and two others have cooked before, but they may not be as fine a cook as Maud was. She was the best cook we've ever had. I must get her back.

"And then there is the problem of ye, Johanna. And I believe I have just come up with the perfect solution for you. Aye. 'Tis exactly what I'll do."

He stuck his head into the small window and grinned. "I'll find ye a husband. I'll get good coin for ye, enough to buy guards. If I must hire them, then I will. Marauders and reivers are always about looking for coin. But until then, ye will tell me where that foolish man is, or I'll cut yer hand off. I was in the mood to chop that lad's hand off, but your fool stopped me. And I was ready. The axe is sharpened and looking for a criminal. I'll chop one of yours off, and if you do not tell me where my dear sweet Meggy is, I'll chop the other one off. And then if you do not tell me what I need to know, I'll chop one of Meggy's hands off when I find her. And if you get away and think I'll not find you, I will. You and Meggy both. Then you'll both pay." He picked up an axe and slammed the blade into the middle of a wooden table. It remained there and Henry chuckled. "It just feels good. Like what my papa felt I'm sure. He loved to cut the heads off the chickens."

She listened, unsure who he was exactly speaking with, but he said nothing else, apparently pleased with what he'd decided.

"Finally, I'll get some answers. Find out who is in the old castle, find a husband for you, and replace Maud and Liam. It will not be so difficult."

She could almost see the grin that crossed his face. "Actually, it could prove to be quite entertaining."

He left, running up the stairs. He was turning daft, of that much she was certain. She thought of poor Davie and her beloved Meggy losing a hand to an axe. She couldn't help but rub her own wrists just at the thought. Children were so innocent and pure until someone taught them otherwise, just as Rohesia and Barnard had done to their two children. Where were Maud and Liam going with that man?

She could only think of one possibility. Was the new man, the one who took Maud and Liam, promising to give them new lives in a new castle? It made sense to her that if he did indeed move into the deserted castle, then he would need a stablemaster and a cook.

And many more.

She had much to learn.

Symon moved below stairs with a smile on his face. It was the first day he'd gotten up with some pleasant thoughts in his head instead of the painful memories that flooded his mind so often of late. He and Finn slept well and got up early to continue their work. Already the hall was much improved because the smell was better and the dust was cleared. Aromas of dried lavender carried throughout the hall, bringing a smile to his lips. His mother had always loved lavender.

The women were busy working in the kitchen, the lads helping, when Gilbert arrived.

Gilbert sent his men back to the curtain wall. "I left the goat and the chickens in the stables. You'll have to find a place for them."

"We can manage, dinnae worry. But please come in, have a goblet of ale and tell me about my neighbors. I'd like to visit them soon." This was one of the first things he wished to accomplish as chief of his clan.

"Ye have two wonderful neighbors besides me,

of course. Flemings are to the north and are fine neighbors. So are the Napiers to the east. Smalleys are to the south, unfortunately."

"So I finally obtain the information I am in need of, only to find out that one of the worst possible neighbors lives south of me." His mind was already coming up with multiple explanations for the man's behavior. He couldn't believe in any of it. "Ye are familiar with Henry Smalley?"

"Aye, we had a bit of a feud a while ago. 'Tis why I stay away from him now."

"Over what?"

"He wanted my castle and I rejected his offer." Gilbert ran his hand through his hair. The man still had a full head of hair for one of his age, though it was a mix of gray and brown hairs.

"What kind of offer was it?"

"He wanted my men to repair the damage the fire made and to repair the curtain wall. Then he would take charge of it, plant their own crops, and they would pay me one quarter of their profits."

"He wanted ye to fix everything?"

"Everything major that was wrong with it. I doubt anyone would have been able to maintain the sizable grounds, but since he insulted me, I didnae consider his offer. He wasnae too happy about it."

"He insulted ye first, then asked for yer favor?" Symon couldn't help but smile at the audacity of the man.

"Aye, he called me an old man. Said I was too old to handle the castle. I didnae take kindly to his opinion." He lifted his chin in defiance of the simple thought of being too old, if Symon were to guess.

"I think ye made a wise decision. I plan to visit him later."

"If he receives ye…"

"He has no reason to refuse me."

Gilbert said, "Best wishes to ye in this endeavor. I'll be inside for the noonday meal."

Symon headed back into the kitchens and said to his sister, "I'm going to meet the neighbors. I'm taking Finn with me. We'll be back in plenty of time for the evening meal. Ye have Gilbert and Liam if ye need help with anything."

Alicia rushed over to his side. "Symon, I wish ye luck and I pray we have fine neighbors, but please dinnae tell any of them why we are here. I dinnae wish to be found by the Chisolms."

"Dinnae worry, sister. I shall be careful. We are a long way from the Lowlands and my guess is the Chisolms have returned to MacKinnon land to finish making it theirs."

She accepted what he said, so he took his leave, wondering along the way exactly how he should handle everything. He thought of his explanation to Liam and Maud and decided it was close enough to the truth that he would stick with it. He had no urge to lie because he knew how easy it was to become tangled in lies, the kind that created a web that wouldn't allow you to be free, as if a spider waited in the wings to snag you in some way or another.

Honesty would be best. He moved toward the

stables and shouted, "Finn, saddle up Nightmare for me."

Finn flew out of the stable. "Ye should see all we've done. 'Tis cleaner and neater than the MacKinnon stables. Come inside."

"Ye've all done a fine job. Where did ye find the extra straw?"

Liam stepped out and said, "Gilbert offered some to us. If ye have any other offers in yer travels, please accept any foodstuffs, straw, or weapons. We can work on starting a group of guards as a few have asked, but we need weaponry and we have no armorer."

"I'll see what I can do. We had many back on MacKinnon land, but I only have my sire's sword now. A few daggers, but no' many swords." How sick he was about all the weapons they lost because of the Chisolms greed and cruelty. A clan had so many valuable parts to it— its people but also its horses, its fertile fields when planted, the skills of their people. Blacksmiths, tailors, and tanners were not that plentiful. "Until we can find an armorer, we may have to purchase some in Dunkeld. Or even back to Perth if we need to."

"Aye, Chief." Liam nodded and spun around without another word. He should correct him, but Finn would tell him not to as he was now the chieftain of his clan. He shrugged his shoulders and thought to leave it be for now.

They headed to Fleming land first and came away with a horse, a goat, and two sheep. He left them in an area on Gilbert's land where they wouldn't disappear, then headed to Napier land.

Again they were treated well, this chieftain a little more direct about Smalleys. "If ye have any trouble with them, I'll loan ye the guards to finish them. There's no' a good one among them. I'd be happy to send them back to England. Why they came here, I'll never know. They dinnae belong in the Highlands. They have no honor." He began to walk away, but then said, "If ye are in need of any straw, just send a man with a cart and I'll send some. And my wife makes mattresses. I'd be happy to gift ye one made of lavender for yer wife."

"Many thanks. I have no wife, but my sister would appreciate the mattress and I shall return to buy the next one when I am able. I would appreciate any help ye can give us and I promise to repay in the years to come."

"Wonderful. When ye send someone for the straw, I'll send the mattress along."

The man didn't offer any other information about the Smalleys, but he did offer Symon a barrel of ale and two bottles of French wine along with a basket full of fresh fruits and vegetables and two loaves of fresh bread. "I send this with wishes for good luck. Know that Highlanders are willing to share with our neighbors and welcome all travelers for a night. It is the honorable Highland way of being neighborly."

"Many thanks to ye, Chief." He left with a good feeling about three of his neighbors. That only left the Smalleys.

He decided to take all the goods home before

he headed to Smalleys. For some reason, if he left any near the Smalleys, he expected something would be stolen before night's end.

And he wasn't expecting any gifts from them.

Finn rode back to get Liam to meet them, while Symon headed back with the livestock, but at their pace. The basket of fresh vegetables and bread he wouldn't leave behind either, but he had to leave the ale to retrieve later.

Liam met up with him, whistling when he saw the livestock. "Yer neighbors are verra generous."

"Our neighbors are. And Napier said we are welcome to straw and a new mattress. His wife makes them. We'll take the one offered and buy one also. We could use a few more, and new is best though most of the ones left behind are no' bad."

"Davie and I can head over later, if ye like."

He passed the vegetables and the wine over to Liam's care, then he and Finn left for Smalley's land. He didn't expect it to be a good trip. "Finn, I'm going to suggest something, and if it's too much for ye, please say so."

"Whate'er ye like me to do, I'll do it. Shall I spy on the bastards?"

Symon couldn't help but smile at the young lad. "Ye dinnae like them?"

"They allow their wee bairns to kick people. 'Tis most wrong. My sire would have made sure I dinnae do it again."

Symon arched his brow at the boy, not wanting any more information. "I wouldn't call it spying, but I'd like ye to see if ye can find Johanna. See if she is being treated well. I dinnae think I'll get the opportunity to speak with her."

Finn grinned, tipped his head back. "My pleasure, Chief. I'll find her. Shall I invite her to come along with us?"

"Ye can, but she'll say nay. I dinnae know why, but Smalley must have some hold over her."

He reached the wrought iron fence around the manor home and was surprised to find the gate open. Dismounting, he sent Finn around the back of the manor while he went directly to the front door and knocked.

The door was answered by a tall thin man he hadn't seen before. The man just glared at him but said nothing. "I'm here to see Henry Smalley. Is he here?"

The man lifted his chin so he could properly look down his nose at Symon. Wherever Smalley found him, he was perfect for his job. No one could hand out disdain so clearly without saying a word better than this man. "Baron Smalley is busy."

Baron. Hmmm. That he didn't know but it did not upset him or change his plans at all. "If I could have but a half hour of his time, I would appreciate it. I am his new neighbor. Moved into Morrigan Castle and would like to get to know my neighbors."

The man stared at him, his beady eyes taking Symon's countenance. "Fine. He wished to know his new neighbor, so I'll give you one quarter hour."

"'Tis all the time I'll need. It should be long enough to get to know each other."

The man led him in through the front passageway into the man's library off to the side. It was a fine chamber, a bookcase with a number of books lining the shelves, a hearth on the far wall with a fine wood mantel above it. Henry Smalley sat behind the desk. "What do you want, Bertrand?"

"This man claims to be your new neighbor, my lord."

Bertrand backed out of the chamber and closed the door behind him. Symon stared at Henry, trying to gauge his reaction, but if he were to wager, it would be that Smalley had no idea he was his neighbor. He also could see the fury in his gaze, thanks to the flames lighting up the chamber.

He would speak and say what he wished to say, then be on his way. There was no reason to waste any time with the man, he just needed to give Finn the chance to locate Johanna. "Symon MacKinnon. Gilbert Morrigan has gifted me with the castle north of yer land. I came to introduce myself and hope to build an amiable relationship with ye."

Henry stood and walked slowly out from behind his desk until he stood a horse length from him. "I recognize you, MacKinnon. The thief. The man who stole my stablemaster and my cook is my new neighbor. I don't have relationships with thieves."

"Stole them? Nay, I didnae. They came willingly

with me and are pleased with their choice. Ye were planning to mistreat the man's son so I rescued him from yer punishment. His wife obviously chose to come along with him. I dinnae know how that's difficult to understand. My apologies but if ye'd promised no' to cut the lad's hand off, I think he would have stayed with ye."

"The lad was a thief, and he was about to get his just due. An apple. The boy took an apple without permission. You cannot steal from a nobleman's family."

"Mayhap he was hungry."

He took a step back and slammed his hand down on his desk. "It was my job to seek justice for the wrong he did me. You interfered. There will be no pleasant relationship between us unless you return them to me."

"Fine, I'll show myself out. I've met Chief Napier and Chief Fleming, and we look forward to a pleasant relationship as neighbors. I dinnae need any help from ye."

"And please do not dare return to my property, MacKinnon."

Symon strode out of the chamber and back down the passageway, but not without checking inside each connecting chamber for a dark-haired beauty.

But she was not there. Not with the sisters, not with the bairns, not anywhere.

What the devil had happened to Johanna?

CHAPTER TEN

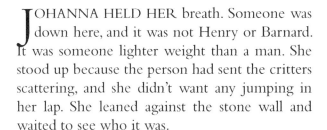

JOHANNA HELD HER breath. Someone was down here, and it was not Henry or Barnard. It was someone lighter weight than a man. She stood up because the person had sent the critters scattering, and she didn't want any jumping in her lap. She leaned against the stone wall and waited to see who it was.

She held her breath, her blood pulsating through her body at a furious pace, one she told herself to calm, but she couldn't, the fear out of control as she thought of all the possibilities. Would it be Barnard with his twisted tendencies? Or Henry carrying an axe? Whoever it turned out to be, she was helpless against them.

She was at their mercy. Completely.

Or perhaps it was her knight. Aldreda was always talking about a strong English knight coming to rescue her from her bland life. He would lift her onto his horse, swear his love for her, and carry her off into the sunset.

How she wished there were someone like that for her.

"My lady." A whisper caught her. She jerked

her face up to the window and saw a lad she didn't recognize staring at her.

Or did she know him? Was he the lad who had been with the dark-haired stranger who'd helped her up from her fall?

"My lady, I'll get ye away from here. Ye can live with us in Morrigan Castle."

She raced to the door, nodding to the lad. "Aye, please. He says he'll cut my hand off if I do not tell him where the cook went or who took her. I truly do not know. I saw the man with dark hair, but I have no idea who he is." She panted, not realizing how nervous she was at the thought of getting caught. "Please. Help me escape. I'll go with you anywhere, anywhere but here with Henry and Barnard and Aldreda and…and…the only ones I liked left and I do not know where they went. And I hate rats! I cannot sleep when there are rats near me. I've had no sleep. No sleep at all." She did her best to hide the tremors in her hand, wondering if she could even walk up the stairs on her own. Little food, no sleep, haunted thoughts, cold temperatures. How long could she survive this form of torture?

"Maud and Liam are with us at Morrigan Castle, a kind chieftain we have. Ye'll be much happier there." He darted around the passageway looking for the key to her chamber. "Where is the key?"

She looked about and pointed, "Over there on the wall."

The lad moved over and tried to jump but it was too high for him.

"Hurry," she said. "And how did you get in here?"

"Through a window at the back, then I snuck down the back staircase. I cannae reach the key." He jumped several times and was able to knock it, but it didn't fall off the nail.

"Hurry. There's a stool over there."

The lad ran to the stool just as the door opened and Smalley entered, bellowing, "I'll kill you, whoever you are." He had a dagger in his hand and ran at the boy with it, the weapon high over his head.

"Run!" Johanna shouted. She couldn't have someone hurt because of her. The lad looked at her and said, "Sorry! I'll be back." He ran down the passageway with Henry chasing him. Barnard and Bertrand both flew down the staircase, searching everywhere for him.

Barnard said, "I'll let you out, my lady. We have plans for you now."

Henry came back, furious. "The wee bastard got away. Who is he?" He moved over to Johanna's cell and opened the door. "Who. Is. He?"

She shook her head, her fear overpowering her. It had to be her lack of sleep that was making her daft. All she wished to do was get away. Scream. Anything but stay in this Godforsaken place she'd been forced to live in without her consent.

"His name, Johanna. I'm waiting."

He took a step closer but she had nowhere to go. "I did not ask him to come. I do not know his name, but he did tell me where he lives."

"Tell me or I'll cut yer hand off right here."

He stepped out of her cell, reached for an axe on the wall, and came toward her. His eyes had darkened, his mouth in a snarl, spittle flying out with every work. "Tell me!" He grabbed her arm, but she yanked it away.

She finally lost all her control, screaming, "Nay, nay!"

Barnard took the axe and said, "Calm down, Henry. Now what did the lad tell ye?"

"He lives at Morrigan Castle. 'Tis where Maud and Liam are." She couldn't stop the shiver going through her at the madness she saw in Henry's eyes. Her hands shook and her teeth chattered from the cold damp cellar.

Barnard's hand settled on Henry's shoulder. "See, Henry. She was honest. I'm sure that's all she knows. She did exactly what you asked so there is no reason to hurt her. Remember the value she represents to us at the moment. Remember the deal you just agreed to. If you cut off her hands, I think the deal would be off. No man wants a wife with no hands."

Henry turned to Barnard and stared at him. "The new arrangement. Of course. I must think of that." He took a few steps back and placed the axe back on the wall. "My thanks for the information, Johanna. That bastard has stolen my castle. No matter. I'll still find a way to steal it for me. You've answered one of my questions. It's all I need for now."

"Good," Barnard said, ushering Henry over toward the staircase. Bertrand headed up ahead of Henry. "You two go on ahead and I'll take her above stairs. We'll give her the news later. First she needs to clean herself up." Barnard smiled at her and winked, his arm wrapping around her shoulders. "Perhaps I'll help ye bathe."

"Nay," Henry barked from the top of the stairs. "You'll not do that while my sister is in the house. Leave her be, but we must get her cleaned up. Her betrothed will be here to see her on the morrow."

"My betrothed? You betrothed me to someone?"

"Aye. His name is Malcolm Chisolm and he's willing to pay fine coin for a beautiful lass. I promised him you are a beauty. I need the money. My coin is dwindling. So you'll go with him at night and come back here during the day to service my sisters as they see fit. Free of charge, of course. It is part of our arrangement."

She knew nothing of the Chisolms. What kind of man was he? Of course, he'd already bargained for his new wife to work for a cruel family with no pay. Or rather, no pay for her, just for himself, if she were to wager.

That posed the question quite differently. What kind of man was he?

She could only pray he was kind.

———◆◆◆———

"What happened, Finn?"

"I found her in the cellars, locked up. But Henry came upon us before I could set her free."

"Get on yer horse. We have to get away." Symon tossed Finn on his horse and slapped the back end of the beast. "Go. And dinnae stop until ye are on Morrigan land."

"Ye mean MacKinnon land?"

Symon mounted with a chuckle. The cheeky lad was always correct.

They were pursued by a poor horseman for a short time, but the man gave up easily. Once they arrived on MacKinnon land, he slowed his horse and whistled for Finn to hold up. Once they were abreast, he said, "Tell me all."

Finn was still out of breath, but he continued, "She was in the cellar, locked in a single cell. She looked much like a prisoner in a dungeon. I would wager she has been there for a day or two at least. She said he threatened to chop her hand off if she didn't tell them who ye were and where Cook was. She said something else too." He slowed his horse, staring up at the clouds gathering in the sky.

"Out with it, Finn."

"She said she was afraid of rats." He thought hard for a moment, scratched his head, then asked, "Do ye think there were rats down there with us when we were in the MacKinnon dungeon?" He looked afraid to ask the question. "I dinnae mind mice. I'm used to them, but not rats."

"I'm sure there were many critters in the cellar with ye. And from the looks of what I observed in the rest of the place, their maid doesnae clean well."

"Or Johanna had to do the cleaning but she was locked up," Finn conjectured.

"Johanna and Maud both did is my guess. Once

Maud finished cooking, she was sent to clean and make beds. I dinnae think the Smalleys tried to do much to keep their help happy. My sire taught me otherwise. Be kind to yer help or they'll leave ye. Those were his words to me." The thought of Johanna having to deal with a rat munching on her beautiful skin in the middle of the night made him want to rip the skin completely off the person who locked her up. "Where was the key, Finn?"

"On the nail. Too high up for my reach but I planned to find a stool so I could reach it. But Henry came barreling down the stairs with a dagger aimed at my neck so I ran."

"I'm glad ye did. Ye are too valuable to lose, Finn. But ye found her and that is the important point of all of this. And Smalley is even more cruel than I would have guessed."

"What will we do, Chief? If we go back now, they'll be waiting for us."

"We will have to wait until we can gather a few other men who can yield a sword. Hopefully, we can get enough men with weapons to go tomorrow eve with us. I'll go to Gilbert and see if he can loan us some men and ask if he has any weapons," Symon said, scratching the back of his neck.

"Can we no' find other men to join us?"

"Maud's sister is coming with her husband. And two men asked at the gates earlier in the morn. Asked if we were taking any into our clan. Liam said aye, but in the future, I must talk with them first. We know we cannae allow all who might try to gain entrance, because some will attempt entrance for ill gain."

"But why?"

"Och, Finn. Some are just born to thievery, but I worry more that Chisolm may hear about us and send spies in. We cannae allow that to happen."

"How will ye know?"

"Instinct. That and talking with our neighbors. Some should know the men in the area. Gilbert probably knows some as they were once in his clan. We'll have to communicate more."

"Ye'll have to invite Gilbert over more to check on our new people."

"Aye, I think ye have the right of it." He couldn't help but sigh. This was not going to be an easy task, starting a clan anew. Inviting new people in. Repairing huts. Finding a blacksmith, a tanner, an armorer. He reminded himself it could take many moons to find just the right people. But a part of him did not accept waiting.

He had a feeling he was going to need all the men and weapons he could find very soon.

CHAPTER ELEVEN

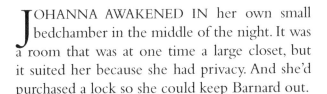

JOHANNA AWAKENED IN her own small bedchamber in the middle of the night. It was a room that was at one time a large closet, but it suited her because she had privacy. And she'd purchased a lock so she could keep Barnard out.

When she'd gone upstairs, Bertrand had ordered a tub brought to her chamber and had it filled with warm water, something for which she was highly grateful, and she intended to thank him appropriately. Even though the tub was small so it could fit in her chamber, the luxury of feeling clean was something she desperately needed. Once the stable lads had removed the tub, she'd relocked the door and fell on her bed into a deep sleep.

She awakened once in the middle of the night to a small voice outside her door. "Johanna, please come for a stroll with me. 'Tis a lovely night outside."

Rohesia's voice had followed Barnard's. "Barnard, stop bothering her and come to bed."

He'd trounced off, lying all the way about just checking to see if she was hale. She'd taken a while to fall asleep after that, but she slept soundly, something she hadn't done in the cellar.

Bertrand had brought her something to eat in the morning and told her to be ready to meet with Henry at high sun. Henry knocked on her door an hour later and said, "Do yourself a favor and clean up because you'll be meeting your betrothed by midday." In the foolish hope that he would be a fine match for her, she did her best to brush her light brown locks until they shined, plaiting them before she chose her outfit.

Now that she had two ruined gowns, one from falling in the dirt the other day and the dirty one from being in the cellar for three days, she had two left to choose from. Selecting the yellow gown that showed off her golden highlights in her hair, she dressed carefully, then scrubbed her face and her teeth.

She didn't leave her chamber until she was called down by Bertrand. Henry smiled, something she rarely saw, and said, "Here she is, Chief, your wife-to-be."

Johanna's belly roiled as she turned to meet her betrothed, a false smile pasted on her face. Henry continued, "This is the Chieftain of Clan Chisolm, Malcolm Chisolm. He's a fine husband for you, Johanna. More than you could have hoped for since you are not of noble blood."

While it was kind of him to remind her, she decided to ignore Henry and curtsied to the Clan Chief, her eyes cast downward. When she lifted her gaze to his, he wasn't even looking at her but instead still conversing with Henry. They talked about issues in the Lowlands, about clan chiefs and feuds, about a clan who hid all their whisky, about the smartest and wisest of all—the Chisolms.

She used that time to take in all there was about her betrothed. He was tall with brown hair that ended at his chin. He had a full beard and was freshly washed. The man actually smelled nice, something she didn't see often in men. Then he turned his gaze to hers and she nearly gasped, but she contained herself.

His eyes were soulless, an empty cavern unlike she'd ever seen before. He smiled, but the smile didn't reach his eyes, instead a hollow expression covered his face as if he wished to hide everything there was about him.

Henry said, "I shall return in a few minutes to discuss our terms. I'll leave you in the library until then." He led them to the library but left the door open.

"My, but ye are a pretty one, Lady Johanna. I guess ye are no' truly a lady, but since ye're to be my wife, ye'll be one by marriage." He smiled as if waiting for her to fall to her knees and thank him for being so considerate of her.

He was a nice-looking man, but she suspected that he didn't have one of the two things she required—a warm heart. Nor did she know if he was honorable. It was all she wished for in a husband, an honorable man with a warm heart. It didn't seem to be too much to hope for, but it apparently was for her.

He held her hand then circled around her with

a smile. "Aye, ye'll do me quite well. Ye look and act like a lady. Are ye sure ye have no noble blood in ye?"

She shook her head, unable to speak yet.

"Ye cannae speak to yer future husband?" He reached for her chin and tugged it up so her eyes met his. And it was a rough tug.

Now she knew. That one movement told her exactly how her life would be with this man.

Rough.

"Aye, I am pleased to make your acquaintance, my lord. How long have you been the chieftain of your clan?"

"Are ye English?"

"My mother was English."

"Ye need to speak like a Scot. We can fix that. Do ye know how to manage a household? Make sure there is food and ale for all?"

"Aye, I believe I can, if not, I am a quick learner. But I was told I would also come back here to take care of Rohesia and her two bairns as I've always done."

He chuckled. "Ye will for a short time, but once I get ye with child, my first-born son, ye'll stay home. Ye are a virgin, are ye no'?"

She dropped her gaze to try to hide her blush. "Aye."

Henry returned and said, "Well, does she suit you? She should, as you can see, Johanna is a fine-looking maiden. If she does not, if she's too sharp with her tongue, I'll see that she fixes that."

"I'm no' concerned about that. If she is, I'll fix it." Then he chuckled and gave her cheek a sharp slap, something that stung and infuriated her though she said nothing. "And I'll knock that temper out of ye too, lass."

She dropped her gaze because she didn't wish to look at the man. Did not wish to talk to him either.

He nodded to her and stepped back. "I'll see ye in a sennight when we marry, Johanna. Until then." He moved toward the door but then stopped when he reached Henry. "Just so we're clear, Smalley. No coin will change hands until I see that she is indeed a virgin. If there's no blood on our wedding day, there will be no coin."

He left, whistling when he closed the door.

She had seven days until she'd be living in a hell worse than the present one.

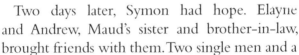

Two days later, Symon had hope. Elayne and Andrew, Maud's sister and brother-in-law, brought friends with them. Two single men and a husband and wife. Three of the men wished to be guards and one had learned the skill of roofing.

Gilbert had sent over three other families who he said would be good, loyal clan members. They'd belonged to Clan Morrigan before they left the castle and were anxious to join in with all their activities. One had been learning to be a blacksmith, something of which they were in great need. The cottages inside the wall now had all had their roofs repaired and the men worked on the inside to ready them for use, but mostly it was up to the women to clean and make the huts livable. Furniture had been rearranged and they found more than they needed in the cellar of the keep. They only had five huts, but two of the families with no bairns had agreed to stay in the hut with two bedchambers until additional cottages could be built.

Word had traveled that Clan Chisolm was making its way through the Highlands looking for people who'd wronged them.

Symon knew it should be the other way around, but he kept his presence low, sending others to the market at Dunkeld for supplies, though they now had a garden to tend and had cleared out some fruit trees from Morrigan's time.

Symon had started training the men with their swords. A few had their own and he purchased several more from Dunkeld. He needed to build their guards so they could protect their castle when they were forced to. He stopped what he was doing when he noticed Alicia and Finn going outside the wall with Gilbert and one of his guards.

"Something wrong?" Symon asked.

Alicia strode directly to him. "Symon, I need to know how to protect myself. Gilbert said one of his guards is a trained archer, so he is going to teach me how to use the bow. He'll teach Finn as well, if ye dinnae mind."

"Nay, I think 'tis a great idea."

Finn came up behind her and said, "Ye approve, Chief?"

"I do. And also, when ye return, I wish to train ye with my sling. The blow of a small rock right between the eyebrows can be mighty powerful. Mayhap ye noticed back on MacKinnon land."

"I did," Finn said. "Davie, I gave him a dagger so he could cut his bindings, then he found his old slinger and hit the Chisolms in the head. Knocked them out quickly. I dinnae know it could be done with such small stones. How did ye learn that, Chief?"

"I practiced when I was yer age. And it only works with the right-sized stone to the temple. Any other place will just make them angry. I'll show ye where to hit yer enemy properly."

"Me too?" Davie asked, directly behind Finn.

"Aye, slingers are easy to make. Then we must find small round rocks to be perfect weapons."

The group moved on, Gilbert mounting his horse while the others walked. "I may go home for a wee bit, then return. I'll get them started."

Finn whistled and the two hounds followed them. "Hunter, we may need ye, and ye can help us hunt later.

Davie ran over to Shadow and gave her a big hug. "I love yer dogs."

Time passed quickly. Symon finished with his group who were progressing well when he saw Finn returning with a bow over his shoulder and a wide grin on his face. "I can help now."

"Indeed, ye can. I'm going to teach ye another way."

Alicia helped them find the exact right cloth to use as a slinger, then the three of them left in search of the perfect sized rocks. "They need to be symmetrical or evenly distributed. If they are really crooked, they may go more in one direction than the other."

Once they finished, he took them to the top of the curtain wall where they practiced firing at a boulder outside the wall. The sound of happiness came when a loud clink resounded, telling them they'd hit the right boulder.

Finn jumped up and down after one loud clink. "Finn, I do believe that was the wrong boulder. Try aiming again." He did as Symon suggested and hit the right boulder, but then he paused, looking off into the distance. "Is that no' Gilbert coming our way? He looks like he's in a hurry, does he not?"

The three paused while Gilbert headed straight toward them on the tower. Symon didn't like the expression on his new friend's face. "Lads, I'm going down to speak with Gilbert. Go find a hiding place for yer slingers in the stable and hide yer stones too. It took a long time to choose those. Find a wee sack for them." The two bounded away while Symon made his way down the staircase at the corner.

Gilbert waved to him, but he did not smile. He dismounted and motioned him over where they could not be overheard, some men practicing their sword skills a short distance away.

"Ye are no' going to like this." The man's eyes narrowed and he crossed his arms.

"What?" Symon had no guesses except he had an odd suspicion that it had something to do with Johanna.

"Johanna is betrothed, and the marriage is to take place in a sennight."

"Aye, I feared that would happen. Who is the lucky man?"

"Malcolm Chisolm."

CHAPTER TWELVE

SYMON THOUGHT HIS head would explode. Malcolm Chisolm had proposed marriage to Johanna and she accepted?

"And before ye start guessing, I'll tell ye what I've learned. It was forced on her. She had no say in the matter, and Henry Smalley will make a fine profit. The dowry goes to him, not to Chisolm. He basically sold her to Chisolm, who will move her into the Lowlands after a moon or two. She has some obligation she must do until she is carrying. Then that agreement is off, and he will take her south."

"Why Johanna?"

Gilbert shrugged his shoulder. "I have never met the lass, but she must be a lovely woman if she's attracted both ye and Chisolm."

"She's yer neighbor. Why have ye never met her before?" Symon was shocked at this revelation.

"Johanna was sold to the Smalleys two or three years ago. She hasnae been there that long. I dinnae visit anyone unless I must, but if I do, 'tis no' the Smalleys. I learned long ago to leave them be."

"How long ago did ye leave here?" Symon asked, indicating the castle.

"Around twenty years ago. Something like that. I've stopped counting because 'tis irrelevant. But it has been long enough to leave some dust all about in the castle, aye?"

"Aye." Symon couldn't think on anything else. Now he was preoccupied trying to come up with a way to get Johanna away from Chisolm. He would not allow the poor lass to be forced into a marriage she didn't want. Finn had said she wished to go with him.

"Pardon me, Gilbert, but I must go chat with some of my men."

Liam asked, "A problem, Chief?"

"Aye. A situation that I must stop."

Finn came running. "I'll help. Whatever 'tis."

Davie was behind him. "Aye, I can help too. As long as I dinnae have to see the Smalleys again I can help."

"It will probably involve the Smalleys, Davie. Mayhap next time for ye. Stay here and help protect the castle while we go."

"All right. I can protect."

Symon looked to Liam and Finn. "We must make a plan, and we will put it into action after the sun goes down."

"This eve?"

"Aye, this eve. Meet me here then, and make sure ye are wearing dark clothing."

Symon strode back toward the keep. He would get a wee bit of rest because he'd made a plan. If they failed this eve, they had six more nights to be successful. He would not stop until he was able to get the woman away from the Smalleys.

He slept fitfully, but he awakened just as the sun dropped, making his way out to the stables, dressed all in dark clothing as he instructed the others to do. He was taking five guards with him, including Liam, and Finn with the dogs.

They left and discussed their plan along the way, all agreeing on the details, then it was settled. "Any questions?" Symon asked. He and Liam, along with the two boys, would be the major players in this rescue attempt.

"What will ye do with her once she's free?" Liam asked. "Do ye have any special plans for her?"

"Nay. Why do ye ask?" Symon hadn't thought about it. True, she stirred feelings in him he hadn't had in a long time, but he was too busy to think about marriage at this point in his life. Perhaps in two years when he was thirty.

"Some of the guards are looking for a wife. Ye say she's a beauty and no' of noble blood, aye?"

"True."

"Then one of them will speak for her if ye dinnae mind."

Symon had the sudden urge to bark out one command. *Mine.* But he didn't say anything. The thought that others would want Johanna hadn't occurred to him yet. He knew he had to consider the possibility. "No' right away. We need to allow the lass to settle. She's been treated cruelly by the Smalleys. She was in the cellar last eve locked up and living with rats. The mother of the bairns she cares for likes to kick her. Leave her be for a fortnight at least. Please advise the men I wish for her to be left alone for that much time. No advances."

"Seems fair enough. She can adjust to living here or will she go home?"

"She has no home, so I suspect she'll stay."

Finn said, "Where do ye think she is sleeping now? Still in the cellar? Is that where ye'll go looking for her?"

"Nay, Maud said her chamber is above stairs, so I'll go there first. I dinnae believe Malcolm would allow her to continue to be mistreated, and I would also wager that Henry Smalley would be easily intimidated by Malcolm Chisolm. I think he'll leave her be for one sennight."

"I would say ye are correct," Liam said. "Henry Smalley is the kind who orders women around easily, but not men so much."

Once they arrived, Symon made a motion for the group to quiet. They tied their horses loosely outside the fence but in a hidden spot where they could easily gain access to them. "Are ye ready, Finn? Now do yer best to distract them but dinnae antagonize them. They will pull out daggers if ye anger them enough. Ye just need to be loud and obnoxious. They'll all gather around."

"Are ye sure of that, Chief?" Finn asked.

"I am. Those are the type of people the Smalleys are." Symon patted Finn's shoulder, then said, "Go ahead, get ready, but give us five minutes before ye let the dogs loose."

Finn nodded, so Liam and Symon moved

around to the back of the house. They would use the back door, hope it was unlocked, then head upstairs. It was said her chamber was directly across from the staircase so they should be able to find it easily.

They made it to the back entrance, then waited to hear the distraction they were waiting for. The sound of barking dogs caught them quickly, surprising him as to how loud and fierce the two hounds sounded.

The two animals barked and ran in circles. Finn started yelling at the animals. "Stop. Ye dinnae belong here. Ye must come home with us right now!"

The plan was for the dogs to run all through the courtyard in front, which meant Finn had to throw sticks or pieces of food around the yard to get them to keep moving. Anything to draw the men out of the manor home.

Henry Smalley came barging out of the door, something Symon could hear from the upper floor. They'd just climbed in through one of the back windows, so he gave Liam a small push. "Go, they are busy."

He heard the conversation going on between the Smalleys and the lad. "What the devil are you doing here on our property?"

"Our dogs ran away. Ye must have fed them. Leave them be so I can take them home."

"We did not feed them."

Bertrand came out and yelled, "Get your dirty arse back home. You do not belong here. You have no noble blood in you at all."

"Close yer mouth, ye old man. Ye are too old to know anything." Finn's strong voice carried to them, and Symon had to smile. He sounded like a true spoiled brat and a lad who was too mouthy.

"What the hell did you just say to Bertrand?" Barnard came out to join Henry and Bertrand.

Henry sniped with a grin, "He said Bertrand was too old to know anything." Then he turned to Finn. "You are a young rapscallion and I do not appreciate anything you say. Get your barking dogs away from here, then take your leave or I'll call the sheriff on you."

"Ye are all too old to fight and 'twill probably take ye half the day to figure out how to call the sheriff." Finn's taunting was perfect. Liam's wide grin told Symon he enjoyed hearing the lad play his part so well.

"You ungrateful cur. I'll slap those wise remarks out of you," Henry said, chasing after Finn.

Finn said, "Surely ye are a big enough man to go after the bigger of the two, or do ye have to go after the bairns?" He held his arms out to taunt the man, a wide grin on his face.

He heard the wives running down the staircase so he moved over to the door he thought to be Johanna's and knocked lightly. "Johanna, come. We must go. We can get ye away from here safely, and ye'll no' have to marry Malcolm Chisolm."

The door flew open and there stood Johanna in her night rail. "Truly? Would you please repeat what you said?"

"Aye, get dressed or throw yer mantle on while I repeat it all. We dinnae have much time."

She nodded and spun around while Symon repeated himself.

Johanna looked back at him and said, "I accept. My thanks to you. I'll be quick." She grabbed a sack from under the bed, tossed a few things in it, then put on her shoes, threw a gown over her head and grabbed her mantle. "I'm ready. Lead the way."

He took her sack and tossed it to Liam, while Symon took her hand to lead her in the darkness. "We have to go out the back. The rest are all out front arguing with a lad," he whispered to Johanna. "The lad I sent earlier to find ye."

"I hope he can get away. They'll try to punish him severely."

"He'll get away."

Henry Smalley's voice carried to them. "I recognize you. You are the lad who was in my cellar. Wait until I catch you!"

Liam looked at Symon and said, "We have to hurry. He recognized Finn."

They grabbed the horses, Liam mounting on one and heading straight for the group. Symon lifted Johanna onto the horse and mounted behind her. "Hang on, my lady, and cover yer ears." Then he let out a shrill whistle and the hounds came running.

Finn tore out from the front of the manor home, so Liam approached and scooped Finn up, landing him in front of him on the horse. "Until later," Liam said to Smalley, who looked so furious Symon thought he might hurl everything from inside his belly across the courtyard.

Liam and Finn took off while Symon distracted the Smalleys by going in a different direction.

The group took off toward Gilbert's land, the others bellowing behind them, but it took a while before they figured out the reason for their visit.

Smalley bellowed from behind them. "The sheriff will return Johanna to me."

She swung around to look up at him, wide-eyed. "Can he do that? Because if he takes me back, he'll beat me until I cannot walk first. He's verra mean."

"I'll protect ye, lass. Ye have my word of honor."

CHAPTER THIRTEEN

PROTECT HER. THOSE were the best words Johanna had ever heard. This man was honorable and trustworthy. He would do what he promised.

"Where are ye taking me?"

"To the new castle on MacKinnon land. Morrigan Castle. It used to be occupied by Clan Morrigan, but it has been turned into a place for Clan MacKinnon for now. We have nearly thirty new people to start. You'll have yer own chamber and willnae be forced to take care of anyone's needs but yer own."

She looked at him in awe. How could he promise such a thing? "Many thanks to you and your helpers. I appreciate it. You do not understand what was to come for me."

"Aye, I do."

"You do?"

"Aye. Malcolm Chisolm was supposedly betrothed to ye, and I dinnae think that was right. Ye would no' have been happy married to him. He's a cruel, heartless bastard."

"Thank you," was all she could get out before she fell against him, the tears of gratitude finally falling. The man was as warm as the biggest hearth she'd ever seen, so she leaned against him and allowed him to wrap his heat around her, something she needed so desperately after her time in the cellar.

She said nothing as they traveled through the forest in the dark, grateful they knew their way, the deerhounds running alongside of them. If he slowed, she feared they'd be stopped, so she silently prayed they would make it to their castle, wherever it was. Anywhere that she would be safe from Henry Smalley and Malcolm Chisolm.

When they approached Morrigan Castle, she was sure of it because the torches lit up the area, making it appear magical. Was this to be her place? A place where she could belong? A place to call home?

"This is a large castle."

"Aye, this is Morrigan Castle. Do ye know Gilbert Morrigan?"

"Nay, but I like the name." They moved through the gates and the guards dismounted and closed the gates quickly. "Were we followed?"

"Nay. But now that we dinnae have to worry about being followed, I have to ask ye about what we spoke of. Is it true ye were betrothed against yer will to Malcolm Chisolm?"

"Aye. I met my betrothed, but I did not like him at all. He had soulless eyes." He reached up for her and helped her down, stopping for just a moment to gaze into her eyes.

"Ye have the bluest eyes, Johanna. Ye are no' hurt, are ye?"

She blushed, enough that he could see her red cheeks deepen in the dark. "Nay. I just met him. Our marriage was to take place in six days."

"I suspect he may appear at our gates on the morrow."

"I hope you are wrong, but I promise to stay inside. Far, far away from any visitors."

He took her hand and led her inside the keep. She didn't mind because it was dark, and she had no idea where to go. The only thing she ever lived in was a small hut and the ugly manor home of the Smalleys.

The keep was majestic. Inside, a blazing fire burned in a huge hearth at the end of the hall. Two women came to greet her, coming from their seats in front of the hearth.

Symon came up next to her. "I am Symon MacKinnon. This is my sister Alicia, and this is Maud. Ye know her, I believe. She came from the Smalleys."

Johanna broke into a wide smile and said, "My dear, Maud. You are happy here? And dear Meggy?"

"Aye. Liam and Davie are here also. Ye probably saw Liam on the way. He helped to rescue ye from Henry."

"We traveled quickly. I thought it was Liam. He seemed happy to be along with us."

Symon said, "They were no' allowed to speak on the way or the way back. We had to make sure we traveled without delay in case we were followed. I just wished to get ye inside the gates. Then I knew ye were safe."

"Many thanks to all of you. I am grateful more than you can know."

"You speak like the English."

"My mother was English."

Symon said, "I hope to talk with ye on the morrow. Until then, Alicia and Maud will help ye to yer chamber."

Alicia said, "We can take ye now if ye like. Welcome to Clan MacKinnon."

"Many thanks to you. I am Johanna Murray. If you do not mind, I'd like to warm myself by the fire first." Symon led her to a chair, moving it close to the hearth, then he found a blanket for her in a basket nearby before he banked the fire, putting more wood inside.

"Are ye warm enough, my lady?"

"Aye, many thanks to ye. Do you really believe Malcolm Chisolm will come for me?"

He sat on a stool that he set in front of her. "Aye. I know the Chisolms. They are a proud lot, and they will take whatever they think they deserve. Ye said ye met?"

"Aye, briefly. But enough for me to know he is not an honorable man like you are, Symon MacKinnon." Symon smiled. He had the whitest teeth and looked even more handsome when he smiled. She was drawn to this man, and it happened as quickly as it took her to wish to be far away from Malcolm Chisolm.

Why? What was it about this man? She had an inkling it was more than just honor, but it was also something she didn't understand yet. But she would, in time, she told herself. Especially if she found herself living in a place where she didn't feel threatened all the time.

"Nay, Chisolm is no' honorable at all. 'Tis an understatement actually. He will take what he thinks is his, and if he feels that way about ye, he will do whatever he can to remove ye from here. I willnae allow it."

On the morrow, she would let him know how appreciative she was of his kindness. But her belly rumbled because she hadn't eaten in so long and she was tired. Her eyes were drawn to the side table where a basket of cheese sat next to a goblet of wine.

His sister caught her looking. "Would ye like something to eat? We dinnae have much, but we are happy to share what we have," Alicia explained. "This is new for us. We just moved in less than a sennight ago. We are grateful to our neighbors who have helped us get started with some livestock and some food stuffs."

"Not from the Smalleys, I'm sure. They are too selfish." She took a hunk of cheese and filled the goblet halfway. "I am always hungry. I was given porridge to break my fast and vegetable broth for supper. This looks heavenly."

"They didn't feed ye well, that much I know," Maud said. "I treasured the few times we were able to talk in private, but it didnae happen often. I believe ye will be happier here. We are. We work hard but now 'tis a pleasure."

Symon said, "We hope ye will stay and consider this yer home, Johanna."

Johanna looked at his hopeful face, but she was more confused than ever. "Truly, I do not know where I belong." Perhaps it was time to go back to her parents and find out why they sold her.

Or would they sell her again?

When Symon awakened the next morn, he was pleased at what had taken place last night and what they'd accomplished. He expected to hear from the Smalleys sometime today and possibly from Malcolm Chisolm. When the bastard learned that Johanna was taken away from the Smalleys, he would come to try to claim her. There was no doubt in his mind that Malcolm would appear, the only question was when.

Perhaps he needed to ask Gilbert for some support and extra guards. Or he could let Clan Napier know or Clan Fleming possibly. They could send guards to assist him. He'd just spoken to Liam about keeping someone on watch for the entire day, that being the most important task. He decided to break his fast, then considered sending a missive to Gilbert. Strolling back to the keep, he was surprised at how he felt. This was the first day he'd had a remote sense of happiness.

Just because of the woman inside.

When he entered the great hall, he was surprised to see Johanna sitting at a trestle table by herself, so he moved inside to speak with her. "May I join ye, my lady?"

"Aye, but Symon, you need not call me by that term. I am not of noble blood. Surely you are aware of that. I am from the working class. A peasant meant to serve the nobles. I expect that if I choose to stay, you will find work for me. May I stay for a fortnight while I decide what I am to do next? I will help out where I can."

"Aye," he said, sitting across the table from her and setting a loaf of bread down between them. "Staying for protection might be the best decision. I know enough about the Chisolms to know that Malcolm will come for ye."

"He will? Will he not consider that my leaving means I am not interested in the marriage?"

"On the contrary, whatever deal he made with the Smalleys, I'm sure it involved the transfer of coin. If he paid Henry already, he either deserves its return or deserves to have ye back. Though I shall be clear in saying that I'll not allow that to happen."

"You will protect me from Malcolm?"

"Aye. He is a monster." Hell, but she looked so small and innocent sitting in the middle of the hall. Feisty was the word he'd used when he'd seen her in Dunkeld, but now she looked exhausted, as though beaten down by her tribulations. That did not sit well with him. He grabbed a small loaf of bread from the side table, grateful to see anything there at the present time. He offered her a hunk, but she declined.

She folded her hands in front of her on the table. "I sensed it when we met, but how do you know of his character?"

Symon decided it was time to tell her the truth. And if it all traveled through the members of his clan, he would not worry about it any longer. "The Chisolms attacked my clan in the middle of the night when we were in the Lowlands. They killed my parents along with my two brothers. There were many others of my clan who lost their lives also. I saw the bodies strewn all over our land, bleeding on MacKinnon soil. I never had the opportunity to bury my family members."

Johanna gaped at him. "I am shocked. Would they not have to answer to the sheriffs? To our king? Can you not get satisfaction?"

"Someday I would like to ask the sheriff of our burgh, but it appeared to me that the Chisolms were given the right to overtake our land for some reason. I hope to seek my own justice someday."

"How did they get in? Did you not have a curtain wall and guards?"

Symon sighed, the true guilt of that night still weighing heavily on his shoulders. "The Chisolms tell me that I allowed them in. That I was deep in my cups and took my horse for a run, leaving the gate open. That was when they came inside, ready to fight. Our guards were no' well prepared and we were sadly outnumbered. We had many guards deep in their cups also. It cost them their lives. Such a sad state of affairs, but I didnae recall any of it until I found myself in the dungeon of our castle. Locked up in my own home."

"I'm so sorry for the ordeal you had, but you know that people with no honor lie frequently. I suspect Malcolm is capable of many lies. It may not have been you at all. Perhaps you should go back and see someday. Speak to the sheriff in your burgh."

"I may choose to do that, but my priority is getting this keep going. I gave my word to Gilbert that we would help repair this keep and clean it up, make it close to what it used to be. I've invited many to join us here, and I may decide to relocate my clan here in the Highlands. The ones who have joined us are willing to work and are excited to be here. I can offer my protection once I am able to build the number of guards. My work is here for now. I'll no' go back on my promises to the good people who have chosen to join me here."

"I understand." She fiddled with the piece of bread in front of her, her blue eyes telling him she was as confused as she'd ever been in her life.

He reached across the table and covered her hand with his. "Johanna, I'll do whatever I can to help ye. The Smalleys and Malcolm Chisolms are bullies, the mean serpents who crawl the earth looking for others to abuse. I cannae stand by and allow it. I promised ye I will protect ye and help ye find a way, whatever it may be. Ye may take all the time ye like to think about yer purpose. Talk with my sister and Maud. This is new for them also. Ye need no' rush yer decision."

"My thanks to you, my lord." She blushed a bit and gazed up at him, a slight misting of tears fighting to be let out, but she didn't allow it. Instead, she lifted her chin and stood from the table. "I think I'll go into the kitchens for some broth this morn. Do you think they have any? I know you are limited."

"I cannae promise, but Maud is in there working hard with her daughter Meggy. You know them well so go see what she has."

She stood with a smile, smoothing her skirt. "Perhaps I'll help them chop vegetables this morn."

He watched her go, the soft sway of her hips mesmerizing his thoughts of the lovely Johanna Murray. A voice pulled him out of his thoughts.

"Symon, something sweet has caught yer eye, I see."

He whirled around, embarrassed to be caught staring at the lady. He nodded to his friend. "She is lovely. Good morn to ye, Gilbert. Ye are ahead of me. I was about to send ye a message."

"No need. Word already reached me. I brought some fresh bread, some dried meat, and cheese in case ye arenae up to using the kitchens yet." He set the food on a side table, bringing half a loaf to set in front of Symon. "Ye took a chance and brought her here, now the question is how exactly will ye defend her? Ye know he'll follow her here."

"'Tis true. I was going to ask to borrow a few guards, mayhap do the same with the Flemings and the Napiers. If I must, I will." He waved to Gilbert to join him at the table.

Gilbert said, "Allow me a moment to speak to my men. I'll return quickly for a bite to eat." He headed out the door at the same time as the door in the back opened.

The sound of laughter carried through just before Maud entered with Meggy and Johanna behind her, the lilt of her voice enchanting Symon unlike any other sound.

Then Johanna sneezed, the highest-pitched, most delicate sneeze he'd ever heard.

Out of the corner of his eye, he noticed that Gilbert had stopped in his tracks, turning around to stare at the lasses entering from the back.

Johanna sneezed again, a sneeze unlike any he'd ever heard. Something distinctly Johanna.

Symon turned back around and couldn't take his gaze away from Gilbert simply because the man was frozen. Unmoving, his jaw was slack as he stared at the women. He took two steps forward and stopped.

"Moira?"

Symon stared at Gilbert, unsure what to do at the moment. Moira was the name of his wife's mother and his daughter. His dead daughter.

"Moira?"

The three females stopped their laughter and stared at Gilbert, unsure of what he was asking.

He needed to take charge of this situation quickly before Gilbert made it too much for Johanna. "Gilbert, this is Johanna. We rescued her last eve from the Smalleys. She was going to be forced into marriage with Malcolm Chisolm. A man no one should have to marry. I'm hoping she'll choose to stay here with us."

Gilbert didn't speak, instead moving forward as if in a trance, ignoring everyone and everything except one—Johanna.

When he was a horse length away from her, his hand came up and stopped in midair. "My word, ye are the spitting image of yer mother. Moira? This cannae be, can it?" He looked at Symon and whispered, "She looks like my Moira would."

Johanna shrunk back from him. Symon said, "He willnae hurt ye, Johanna. He had a daughter long ago and lost her. Ye must look like her." Then he turned to his friend. "Gilbert, ye are frightening the lass. Please explain yerself."

Tears misted his gaze as his hands fell to his side. "What is yer name? Yer full name?"

"Johanna Mor Murray."

"Yer parents? What are their names?"

"John and Joan Murray."

"John Murray? Was he an armorer? Did he make weapons? Knives, swords?"

She nodded, her gaze jumping to Symon's occasionally for support. He reached for her hand and held it, hoping she would feel better about the odd inquisition.

"Just one favor, I ask of ye."

She didn't agree so Symon said, "Ask it and she'll let ye know if she agrees. Even I am wondering what ye are about, Gilbert."

"She looks like my daughter would, just like my wife. She was supposedly the one who died within a fortnight of her birth. I never saw her body, never saw her body go into the ground. I could not bear to watch. But she did have a birthmark, and it was exactly like her mother's. I wish to see if she has it." He looked from Symon to Johanna, who still hadn't agreed to anything.

Instead, she took a step closer to Symon. "Will ye feel any pity for an old man who just seeks clarity?"

"Where is the birthmark?" Symon could hardly turn him down after all Gilbert had done for him.

Gilbert's hand reached around to his neck. "Under her hairline on the back of her neck. She had a red mark there, though many have it, hers was the shape of a star. Just like her mother's."

"May I look, lass?" Symon asked.

She nodded, reaching back to lift her honey-colored plait and turning to give Symon full view of her hairline.

Symon said, "Looks like a star to me. I dinnae think Johanna will mind if ye take a look." He waved to Gilbert, who peeked around and gasped when he saw it as tears covered the older man's cheeks.

Gilbert whispered, "'Tis Moira's mark. I looked at it for near a fortnight." He sat down, looking quite dazed by everything.

Johanna reached for Symon's hand again and gripped it so tightly he didn't know if she would let go. Her voice trembled, but she spoke her mind clearly. "But my parents are the Murrays. I lived with them until he injured his back three years ago, then were forced to sell me a year after that. The birthmark must be a coincidence. I never heard of you or your wife."

Symon knew this was difficult for both of them. Gilbert clearly thought Johanna could be his daughter, and Johanna had no comprehension of what had happened to Gilbert twenty years ago. He had to remind himself that Johanna owed Gilbert nothing. If she wasn't interested in pursuing the truth in this matter, he could not force her to be involved. "Do ye know the Murray's, Gilbert? Have ye any idea how it could have happened?"

Gilbert nodded, walking away from the group to pace, his words scattered but quite convincing. "The Murrays lived in a hut down by the river. It overflowed that year and they lost everything. Their home, the weapons he'd worked on. Everything. She'd tried to have a bairn on several occasions but failed. When their home was destroyed, he came to me and said they were leaving, going to work on weaponry. I asked him where they were going, he said he had no idea. Said they would know it when they saw it. I never saw them again."

"This was before or after Moira was born?" Johanna asked.

"After. In fact, I believe Joan was one of the wet nurses we used because she'd just lost a bairn so she had milk at the ready for ye when yer mother died.

"So you are suggesting they are not my true parents?"

"'Tis exactly what I am saying. Once my Elspeth passed, mayhap they stole ye away. If I recall, it would have happened on the same day, but I never considered they would commit such a despicable act. There was a funeral held, but I could not attend. I was so devastated that I barely left my chamber. I trusted what the healers told me."

"Just to be clear, you are suggesting that you are my true sire, that the Murrays were not?" Her color paled considerably. After all she'd been through, perhaps this was too much for her, would eventually drive her away.

Symon could see the panic in her eyes, the fear, the uncertainty. Would she bolt as soon as she as the opportunity arrived? And if she did, where would she go?

Certainly not back to the Smalleys. From what he knew about Johanna, there was only one place she could go—back to her parents. But if she went to her parents, wouldn't she have to ask some questions after this possible scenario had come about?

Gilbert said, "Ye look exactly like my wife. You do not look like either of the Murrays."

She cleared her throat and stared at the floor. "Nay, I did not. I often wondered where I got my lighter brown hair. John's was red and Joan's was black as night."

"And yer eyes are blue like Elspeth's."

She shook her head, her hands kneading in front of her. "Neither of the Murray's have blue eyes."

"When was the last time ye saw them? A few days ago?"

"Nay," Johanna said. "They sold me to the Smalleys. They told me they ran out of money and had nothing else they could do so they sold me to be a maid to the two sisters. I'm servant to Aldreda and Rohesia Smalley."

"They sold ye to the Smalleys," Gilbert said, stroking his beard and repeating his words. "Lass, if ye can be patient with me, I wish to locate the Murrays and speak with them. And if they tell us exactly what happened, I promise to bring them here so they can explain to ye what happened."

She nodded and said, "I shall remain here."

Gilbert nodded and headed to the door, but then he stopped and spun around to face them again. "I dinnae wish to frighten ye, lass, but I believe ye are the daughter I lost, and I pursue this because I would like to get to know you better, if ye will allow us that chance. But first, I wish to hear the confession from the guilty party. I wish to give ye the proof ye deserve, the truth of what transpired. Ye deserve nothing less than that. I dinnae expect ye to change yer beliefs based on my suspicions alone. I understand I'm sounding a wee bit daft, but I must see this through, Johanna. I promise that I shall return as soon as I have learned the truth."

Symon said, "She will be here. I'll not allow the Smalleys or Malcolm to remove her from here." He didn't wish to tell him how he truly felt.

Johanna belonged here with him. That was the true reason he would keep her here.

CHAPTER FOURTEEN

JOHANNA TURNED TO Maud and said, "May I help you chop vegetables, please?" She peered up at Symon, who looked as confused as she felt. "I'd like to step away, if you please."

"Aye, I'll see ye on yer way, Gilbert." He followed Gilbert out the door.

Johanna rushed into the kitchen and collapsed into a chair. "I do not know what to do." Maud followed her and said to Meggy, "Please get her a cup of warm broth, Meggy. I just put some in the kettle on the hearth. We'll throw the vegetables in later."

Maud knelt down in front of Johanna. "Ye are confused and understandably so. Tell me yer thoughts."

Johanna had so many thoughts she didn't know where to start. She couldn't stop wringing her hands in her lap, staring up at the ceiling to keep the tears at bay. Her parents were not her real parents? They stole her away from her true mother? That meant her entire life was based on lies.

"I've never heard of such a thing. Stealing a bairn away from its mother? It truly happens?"

"Aye, I knew of one mother who lost her son of six moons and stole one from a mother who had eight. Decided the other mother didnae need so many. But she missed her own bairn so much she took the stolen boy back. 'Tis no' right. Did ye have any siblings?"

"Nay, none. They lost some but I know not how many. Would you steal another woman's bairn if you had none, Maud? Help me understand this."

Maud sighed. "I would never do such a thing because I understand the love a mother has for her bairn. But I can tell ye this. I would never… *never*…sell my bairn for any reason. To me, that is the most suspicious behavior of this entire situation. How could yer mother have sold ye to the Smalleys? Did she ever contact ye later to apologize?"

Johanna shook her head, bits and pieces of scattered conversations returning to her. A vision of her mother sobbing while her father consoled her about the bairns they lost. A time when she was little and her mother told her father they had to find a way to color her hair darker. She closed her eyes, her mind going back to many times of confusion in her life, the different situations bubbling out of her mind faster than she wished to contend with at present.

Once she awakened in the middle of the night and her mother was washing her hair with mud. Told her it was a mud bath to make her hair shine special.

She also recalled her mother being furious when she washed the mud out. Johanna had thought it was because her hair hadn't turned shiny, but now she knew better.

Her hair hadn't darkened to match her mother's hair color. Or *Joan's* hair color. Was she her mother or not? Other memories faded in and out as she considered the possibility that she'd been stolen away.

A time when she walked in on her parents' conversation discussing how they could make her stop growing. Her mother had suggested binding her feet together and making her sleep in a box at night. Her father had called her suggestions cruel.

"What is wrong with me?" she'd asked. Her mother had tossed her needlework in the chair and stormed out. That made her feel everything was wrong with her.

"Tell me yer thoughts, Johanna. Gilbert is gone."

The comment came from Symon, who was kneeling in front of her. Maud waved as she and Meggy left the kitchens. She reached for his shoulder as if that one act would steady her, keep this chaos that was her life of late at bay.

"Confused," she mumbled. His hand came up to cup her face, his thumb wiping away each tear as it fell.

"Do ye recall much about yer parents? Talking about yer birth? Anything like that?"

"Nay," she cried, the tears now covering her cheeks as they flowed in buckets. "I recall other things, like the day they tried to darken my hair with mud, the day my mother wanted to bind my feet together to keep me from growing…" She had to stop because her breath hitched so badly.

"Because ye were taller than both of them? Gilbert is a tall man."

She nodded. "And when they wouldn't take me to festivals because I'd be seen. I heard my mother whispering to my father. Heard him tell my mother she couldn't live in the past forever. Once he said no one would ever suspect… Once he swore no one would ever take me away or they'd have to kill him first. I recall Mama saying she promised to stay with me forever, that she'd never allow anything to separate us. I never understood what worried them so. Now I do."

She rubbed the tears from her face so furiously that they flew far away from her and Symon stilled her hand, wiping her tears with a linen square.

"Then before they sold me, my father told my mother it was time to marry me to someone. She refused. Said the truth would come out if I married. Said they would have to move far away. I never understood what they meant by that statement, but it makes perfect sense now. The truth is that they stole me away from Gilbert and my true mother. How did they do it?"

She tipped her head forward, memories refusing to stop no matter how she tried to end them. She recalled staring at both of them and screaming, "What truth? Why won't you tell me what you're hiding? It's time. I'm old enough for the truth, whatever it is."

Her breath hitched and she squeezed Symon's hand so hard she had to apologize to him.

"They sold me to the Smalleys a sennight after I asked them what they were hiding from me. That I knew something was different about me. I screamed at them that I didn't look like either of them, that others teased me because I looked like they adopted me."

"And so they let you go to save themselves," he whispered in her ear.

"Aye!" She fell against him, her chin locked onto his shoulder and her hands gripped his arms as she sobbed for all she was worth. And Symon MacKinnon did the nicest thing anyone had ever done for her.

He held her while she cried.

And listened.

The patient man waited until all her tears were spent. Her head was on his shoulder because they'd stood up together. She whispered, "You are too nice to me, Symon."

He said, "May I tell ye a secret?"

"Aye, please do. You've heard many of mine." She ran her hand up his arm, liking the hardness she felt there, especially in his upper arm. He was all muscle.

"I like that ye are tall. Ye fit me verra well."

She took a step back and looked up at him. "I was shielded from life. At this point, you must understand that. So believe me when I tell you that I'm not sure I understand your comment. What do you mean by 'fit you?'"

"I believe ye when ye say ye are innocent. I

have a verra strong urge to kiss ye, but I fear ye've never been kissed. I dinnae wish to frighten ye or take advantage of ye during a difficult time."

She scowled and shook her head slightly.

"The best way to explain that ye fit me well is to show ye. May I kiss ye, Johanna?"

She didn't know what to expect, but she knew she wanted more from this man—the man full of honor and kindness. "Aye."

His finger lifted her chin and his lips touched hers, oh so softly. He pulled back and gazed into her eyes. "Do ye accept, lass? Would ye like me to stop?"

"Nay. Please do not stop."

He kissed her again and she sighed, her lips parting until his tongue breached her mouth, the tip of his touching hers. His arms fell to her back, caressing her slowly. She had no idea how to react to this invasion except for one obvious response she had.

She liked it. She liked Symon MacKinnon.

She fell against him with a sigh and he let out a low growl, tugging her closer until her body melded against his and she suddenly understood.

Johanna fit Symon quite well.

He ended the kiss and she stepped back, losing her balance a touch, but he righted her with a grin of satisfaction. "Ah, lass. Ye fit me more than quite well. I like that ye are tall because I am. Ye fit me quite perfectly. Now do ye understand?"

She nodded, a wide grin breaking out across her face. But she understood something else that had been missing in her life forever.

Happiness. She'd just experienced a brief touch of happiness and now had a sudden understanding of what love meant.

And perhaps it was time to seek the truth of her parentage. She needed to speak with her parents soon.

CHAPTER FIFTEEN

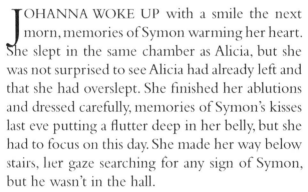

JOHANNA WOKE UP with a smile the next morn, memories of Symon warming her heart. She slept in the same chamber as Alicia, but she was not surprised to see Alicia had already left and that she had overslept. She finished her ablutions and dressed carefully, memories of Symon's kisses last eve putting a flutter deep in her belly, but she had to focus on this day. She made her way below stairs, her gaze searching for any sign of Symon, but he wasn't in the hall.

She greeted Alicia and sat at the trestle table across from her once she grabbed a bowl of oats from the kitchens. "Good morn to you. Have you seen your brother yet?"

"Aye, he said he'd be out training the men and he wishes to keep an eye out for any visitors. Why? Did ye need to speak with him?"

"Nay, I was just curious if the Smalleys or Malcolm had been seen at all."

"I havenae seen him, but 'tis still early. Once ye finish, I can take a walk out with ye. Show ye the grounds of the castle. 'Tis quite lovely. This castle is much larger than our castle in the Lowlands, and this one is built almost completely of stone. The other keep was partially destroyed because it was made of timber. I feel safer here, but ye need to see it all for yerself."

"I would like that."

Alicia chattered on about the cloth she'd bought and what she hoped to do with it. "Have ye sewn at all?"

"Aye. I made all my own clothing, so I'd be happy to help ye with whatever ye need. I was able to grab two gowns before we left, so I am fine for a wee bit. But I spent my life learning needlework, so I'll help sew anything."

"Symon said he ordered more gowns and some bolts of fabric from the tailor. We'll have to return for them."

Alicia put her needlework down and looked at her. "Ye are a beautiful lass, Johanna. I think my brother likes ye. Would that upset ye?"

Not knowing how much to confess, she looked at Alicia and shook her head. "I like your brother too."

Alicia nodded and said, "Good. He's a good man. I love him dearly, but I wish he would find someone. I never gave it much thought when my sire was still alive, but he is the chieftain now. He needs to have sons and daughters."

Maud came in and discussed the meal plan with Alicia, so Johanna became lost in her thoughts. She finally finished her porridge, as much as she could. Her thoughts kept returning to Symon. She'd experienced the most wonderful night, her sleep full of dreams of solid arms and warm lips covering her in many different ways. But then the sweet memories were interrupted with the truth of the situation.

This day or the morrow, she would find out the truth from her parents. Her belly was still unsettled waiting for news from them.

Or were they her parents? And there also was the issue of her betrothed. Would he accept her departure, or would he come flying after her?

She was so wrapped up in her thoughts that she hadn't noticed Symon enter the hall until he was standing directly in front of her. "Oh! I did not notice you."

He feigned disappointment and said, "Ye have forgotten last night already?"

"Nay!" So upset that she may have given him the wrong message, her response came out in a near shout.

He waggled his brow and said, "Good. I have fond memories of my own."

"Is there something wrong? Has Malcolm come for me?"

"Nay, not Malcolm, but I believe we will be seeing Gilbert soon, so why do ye no' get comfortable over by the hearth." He held his hand out to her and she took it, delighting in just the warm touch of their hands.

Once she was settled, he said, "I will return to the curtain wall, but I pledge to ye that if I learn anything about Gilbert, Henry Smalley, or Malcolm Chisolm, I will let ye know immediately."

"Many thanks to you, Symon, for everything. Saving me from Malcolm, holding me while I cried. I'm still as confused as ever, but I feel like I'm finally living my own life and not someone else's."

Once she sat, he settled the blanket over her lap, kissed her cheek. "I'll return in a wee bit."

Alicia joined her once her brother left. "May I sit with ye?"

"I would love to have your company, Alicia."

Symon left and the two were alone.

Alicia said, "I'm sorry to pry, but is there something between ye and my brother?" She leaned toward her and whispered, "Did he just kiss yer cheek?"

"He did." Johanna couldn't stop the instant blush in her cheeks and knowing they betrayed her true feelings, she didn't attempt to lie. "Getting to know a grown man is new for me. Other than the help, I haven't befriended many. He is kind and honorable. What is not to like about Symon? I am surprised he is not married."

"He is of age and my father used to tell him so often. But before we lost our family, Symon liked to imbibe a bit too much. Now I see him drink verra little. That pleases me. I think ye will be a good influence on him. I am pleased to see he is interested in ye, 'tis why I ask. He's my only family left. I feel protective of him, and I'm proud of him for what he is building here. I hope he decides to stay here and no' return to the Lowlands."

"With your help and many others, he is successful. He could not do it alone, but he is hard-working." Then she blushed again and whispered, "And handsome."

"Have ye sorted the other issue in yer mind? I feel so badly that this is all upon ye."

"I have not. The possibility of different parents answers so many questions I've had over the years if it proves to be true. We shall see." She looked at Alicia, wondering how much she should say. This was all new for her, having a friend to confide in, having a man interested in her.

"What?" Alicia asked. "Are ye worried I'll tell others? I give ye my word that what ye tell me is confidential if that is yer wish."

"It is my wish." She thought hard for a moment and then said, "Who would sell their only child?"

"'Tis my first thought. I've heard of families of ten selling one or two, but never an only child. It tells me their feelings are different."

"It tells me their love is not true. I often wondered why I never had friends. In fact, I was ten winters old before I learned what a friend was. We attended a church session, and a wee lass asked me if she could be my friend."

"Oh, that was sweet."

"We never returned again. My mother told her I wasn't allowed to have friends. I asked my mother what a friend was, and she told me I didn't need to know."

The door opened and Symon entered. He came directly to the hearth and knelt down in front of her. "Gilbert has returned with the man who ye think of as yer father, John Murray. Will ye see them both at the same time? I said I would ask, but I might recommend ye see John Murray alone. Or mayhap with Alicia or with me present, but no' Gilbert until ye've heard the words from John's lips."

"That makes perfect sense. I'd like you both to stay, but not Gilbert yet. My thanks for your suggestion."

Symon rearranged the chairs, then stepped out, returning a few minutes later with John Murray, whose shoulders were slumped and he held his hat in his hand. "Greetings to ye all."

Symon said, "This is my sister Alicia. Johanna has asked us both to stay while ye say what ye've come to say. Please sit down."

The man she knew as Papa had aged a good deal. She nodded to him, not knowing what to call him until she heard the truth. He took the chair and paused while Symon settled.

"Papa, if you are my papa, I need to hear the truth. Though whatever you tell me, either way, I recognize that you raised me and loved me through many years. That will not be forgotten."

John said, "Many thanks for that. Your mother, err…Joan, will appreciate those feelings." He paused to stare at her, then let out a long deep sigh before he continued, "Joan and I lost three bairns. The third one was our only lass, and she passed the day you were born. When we heard the Morrigans were seeking wet nurses for their bairn, Joan wanted to help. I thought it would be good for her, but it wasn't. Once she held you in her arms, she didn't wish to let you go so she came up with a plan. Joan stole you away one day, hurrying home with you wrapped in a blanket and said she'd already gone to the garden, dug up our dead bairn, and switched the bodies so no one would know.

"She begged me to help her, said your mother was dead so what did it matter. Convinced me all bairns need a mother, so I went along with it. In fact, by the time I came home, word already passed that they'd found the Morrigan bairn wrapped tightly inside a blanket, dead. You looked much like our bairn, so it was not hard to convince others that it had happened. And I must add to that, you had already grabbed a piece of my heart in that short time. Holding you, why you were a magical bairn. Beautiful." He looked at her, then looked away and stared at his hands again. This was clearly very difficult for him.

"We moved away. We heard later that all had believed you had passed, that Joan's switch had been successful, so we thought we were safe, though I would have moved back to England if forced to just to keep you. You were the shining light we'd been looking for and once you were in our home, I couldn't give you up. We both adored you. Joan was so taken with you that I knew if I returned you that she would lose her mind and I would be alone. So I said nothing.

"I realize it was the wrong thing to do, and as you grew older, we argued about what was the right thing to do. I wanted to tell you the truth once you were old enough, but Joan didn't. Once you started asking questions, we knew we had to do something and the Smalleys came to our house looking for someone to help them in their home. We needed the coin and…" He shook his head, tears misting his wrinkled eyes.

Johanna held her palm up so he would stop. "There's no reason to continue, Papa. I forgive you for what you did many years ago. Tell Mama I feel the same." Then she paused to gather her thoughts before she said the most difficult words. "But what I cannot forgive is selling me to the Smalleys. They've treated me horribly and I felt so unloved, like no one wanted me. I fear those two years have done irreparable harm. I will try to make myself a new life here. I plan to join Clan MacKinnon, and I will acknowledge my true father as such."

She got up to give him a hug and said, "My thanks for loving me for eight and ten years. I just wish you'd loved me a wee bit longer."

She couldn't stay here in front of him. There was a part of her that wished to lash out at him, pummel his chest with her fists, even scream at him. Tell him every indignity and punishment she'd been subjected to by the Smalleys, but she couldn't do it. He looked ashamed enough. So she did what she thought was her only alternative and left for the privacy of her bedchamber. She needed to be alone for a few moments.

Her heart was broken.

Symon didn't want to let her go, but he knew he had to, so he escorted John Murray back out of the keep and made sure he was on his way before he spoke to Gilbert, also explaining to the man how Johanna had ended up with him and not the Smalleys. Once John was gone, he approached his friend. "She was upset, understandably so, so she went to her bedchamber. I think she needs some time alone to absorb what has happened."

"How did she accept it?"

"As regal and graceful as anyone would. She thanked him for their love all those years but said that she wished the love had extended long enough they would not have sold her to the Smalleys, or in so many words. She said she was not treated well there, and the entire situation made her feel unloved. She's hoping to repair those feelings."

"She's a wise woman. They did raise her and did a fine job for the most part."

"I think keeping her hidden for so long probably hindered her growth, but time will tell. Ye accepted it when he told ye the truth, Gilbert, and didn't wring his neck? I ask because I'm not sure how I would have reacted."

Gilbert paced a bit before returning to Symon. "Joan is the one I fault, and she didnae even attempt to see me or apologize. I don't think she feels she owes anyone anything. In her mind she did nothing wrong since Moira's mother was dead. I cannae disagree with someone who says every bairn needs a mother. I agree with that, and I would have been a poor mother until she grew older. But I would have given her my undying love. At this point, there is no sense looking back. I wish to get to know my daughter, but 'tis her choice. I'm no' sure what to call her and that is also up to her."

"You're a wise man, Gilbert. Come inside for a bite to eat. I'm going to check on her and see how she's doing."

They moved into the hall together. Supper was now being served, a vegetable stew, along with bread they'd saved from the day before. There was ale for all because they'd been gifted a barrel from one of the neighbors.

Gilbert joined a table of guards while Symon went above stairs to knock on Johanna's door. "Johanna, I'm here when ye are ready to talk." He took a stool from another chamber and set it in front of her door, sitting down with his back to the door.

He listened to the general revelry over supper while he waited. It gave him great pleasure to see his clan mates happy and hopeful and know that their bellies would be full this eve after a hard day's work. And he prayed he could guide them with half the wisdom his sire had.

Johanna didn't answer for several minutes, but he was a patient man, especially for a woman who was beginning to mean more to him than any other woman had. He wasn't even sure what he wanted from her, except to get to know her better.

When she did finally open the door, she giggled. "You were telling the truth, I see."

He turned around and smiled, then stood, setting the stool to the side of the door. "I am here for ye. Ye've just received some difficult news. Ye must be more than confused."

She said, "Come in, please. I do not know if that is something acceptable unless we are married because I have not been around enough people to know how I'm supposed to act, so please tell me if I am doing something wrong."

"Ye arenae. We are both adults and no one will judge ye. This is our world, not theirs."

He stepped inside but left the door open in case there were any wagging tongues below. "I think ye handled yerself verra well, but I'm no' sure where ye will go from here."

"I feel betrayed, but yet I now have a clarity and an understanding of my life that I never had before. As I move through life and learn how to conduct myself in situations I've never been in before, perhaps my anger with the Murrays will grow, but for now, I am fine." She sighed and paced the room twice before sitting in a chair by the fire. "I wish to get to know my true father. And I wish to learn about my mother. I know the Murrays raised me and I have much to be grateful for, but I have much to make up for as well. Will you help me, Symon?"

"Of course. I know Gilbert is hoping you will accept him, but he recognizes this is all on yer terms because ye are an adult. 'Tis yer decision to make. I think it starts with whether ye wish to be called Moira or Johanna."

"I'll stay with Johanna Mor, but I wish to change my last name to Morrigan. I'm not interested in being a Murray any longer. Does that suit you?"

"Aye, it does and it will please Gilbert, I'm sure."

Liam appeared in the doorway and looked as if he'd seen a ghost.

"What is it, Liam?"

"Malcolm Chisolm is at the gates requesting entrance. He has five guards with him and says he has come for his bride."

"I will be there immediately." He began to leave but then turned to Johanna. "Would ye like a word with yer betrothed, or shall I inform him of all that has taken place?"

"I'd like to go and break our betrothal officially with witnesses, if you don't mind."

He smiled and said, "After ye, my lady. Ye have guts and I do approve." His hand settled on the small curve in her lower back, something that made her feel special. He would protect her against Malcolm. She was certain of that.

"Symon, I've asked you not to call me that name."

"But that was before ye learned that ye are indeed of noble blood. Yer sire is chieftain of Clan Morrigan."

She paused and gave him a small smile. "So be it."

They walked side by side and moved up to the tower near the gate, looking down at Malcolm and his men. The fury in his gaze was evident, his jaw clenched and his fists tight on the reins.

Symon started the conversation, directly to the point was the best with bastards. "Chisolm, Johanna will no' be leaving with ye."

The man looked massive atop his warhorse,

but Symon was more impressive in her eyes. And certainly much more handsome. Even with Symon by her side, she still kneaded her hands in front of her, a nervous habit she wished she could stop.

Malcolm bellowed, "Aye, she will leave with me. She's my betrothed. I paid good coin for her. Johanna, get down here now. I will take ye to the priest and finish this immediately. Dinnae disobey me."

She took a deep breath and leaned forward. It was time to learn to stand up for herself. "Nay, I'm sorry, but I will not be marrying you, Malcolm. My parents, the Murrays, just informed me they stole me away from my birth parents. They sold me to the Smalleys, and Henry Smalley made that arrangement with you, whatever it is. But they did not have the right to sell me, so I am no longer working for them, and I will not honor the betrothal agreement they made without my consent."

"Then who is yer true sire? I'll fix this. I want ye now. No arguments, lass, or ye'll be pricking my temper in a way ye dinnae wish to do." His horse pranced in response to the man's anger.

The gates opened and Gilbert rode out to meet Chisolm with a dozen guards behind him. "Johanna is my daughter, Chisolm, and ye are no' welcome to her. She is of noble blood and will not marry without my permission. I will assist her in choosing her husband. Yer betrothal is done. I will take the information to our king so it is clarified that she is my daughter. Take yer leave. In fact, leave the Highlands and go back to the Lowlands where ye belong. Ye arenae wanted here."

Malcolm's anger was so visible he was nearly spitting. "I'll return after I seek justice for this."

"Ye need to see Henry Smalley about that."

"I will. And then I'll go back to Chisolm land. The land that used to be MacKinnon land. Going to have a chat with yer brother, MacKinnon." He winked at Symon and broke into a wide smile. "He's more of a drunkard than ye. But know that this is no' over."

He turned his horse around and they left.

"Do ye feel better, lass?" he asked after they descended the steps, ignoring the mention that Malcolm deliberately made to goad him. His brother was alive. Which one?

"I do." She smiled, pleased that she hadn't been carried off by that raging beast. "My thanks for your protection. I should speak with Gilbert now."

Gilbert and his men reentered the gates, closing them behind the last guard. He dismounted and Finn took care of his horse, then he joined Symon and Johanna. She could see in his eyes that this was going to be difficult for him. But she also saw something else evident in his gaze, something she wasn't accustomed to seeing. Gilbert loved her the way a father should, something that meant more than she cared to admit. Unconditional love that would always be there for her. She'd had it at one point in her life, but she'd lost it.

"I thank ye, lass, for agreeing to see me. What may I call ye?"

"Ye may call me daughter or Johanna. Either suits me. Johanna Moira Morrigan. I've changed it a wee bit, Symon. I hope you both approve."

Gilbert relaxed, his shoulders dropping while a small smile crossed his face. "I do approve. As my daughter, I will give ye my protection, but I would also like to get to know ye better. Would ye consider staying at my manor home for a short time? I understand ye wish to join Clan MacKinnon and I respect that. Mayhap I'll consider moving back here myself." He made a quick pivot to Symon. "Though ye are renting it for now, it will stay Clan MacKinnon under yer leadership. I'm no longer interested in taking over as clan chieftain. I believe ye will do a fine job at it, Symon. I will give ye my complete support. I hope ye will both agree with my suggestion."

They both waited to hear from Johanna, who thought for a moment, then said, "I would like that. And my guess is that Symon has some other business to attend to if I understood things correctly." She glanced over at him and caught sight of a vein on his forehead that stood out prominently, a sure sign that he had indeed heard something upsetting.

She had much to learn about this man she was falling in love with, but she had the time. She reached for his hand, unsure of any other way to give him her support in this difficult situation.

He glanced at her, a look that went straight to her heart, a bit of appreciation combined with a wee bit of worry. Normally he was a solid and confident man. But not at the moment. He held her hand and squeezed it, not letting go. In fact, his thumb rubbed the skin on the back of her hand.

Such a small touch of caring nearly brought tears to her eyes. She took a step closer, a need of this man blossoming inside her.

Gilbert said, "I believe ye are correct, Johanna. Did ye know one of yer brothers survived, Symon?"

"Nay, I didnae, and obviously, I will investigate. I'll be heading to the Lowlands on the morrow. It pleases me and eases my burden to know that she is under yer protection while I'm gone. Though I'm sure I know where I'll find the rest of the Chisolms, I'm unsure after that interaction which way Malcolm will go. I will look for him on my journey."

"I expected ye would."

They headed back inside as a group, but Symon couldn't stop his mind from going back to the important fact he'd just learned.

Which brother was alive?

CHAPTER SIXTEEN

SYMON AWAKENED THE next day near dawn. He headed below stairs to get ready to leave for the Lowlands. Alicia and Johanna were breaking their fast, sitting across from each other. He moved over to the table, kissed each one on the cheek as a greeting and took the seat next to Johanna. Meggy came out of the kitchens and set a large bowl of porridge in front of him. "Many thanks to ye, Meggy."

The lass giggled and ran back to her mother in the kitchens. Then she stopped and spun around, returning to his side. "I like it here much better." Then she ran off, skipping her way to the kitchens, a sure sign of a happy bairn.

"I'll only take what dried meat ye can spare and a hunk of the dark bread to head south with, Alicia. Have we enough?"

"Aye, there's plenty of dried meat. I'll fill a sack for ye when ye are ready."

"My thanks. I promise to return with what foodstuffs I can find in Dunkeld again."

Alicia said, "Symon, I've thought verra hard about your news that one of our brothers survived, and I cannae decide exactly how I feel. I feel terrible for even speaking it but I'm hoping 'tis Boyd. We were always closer and…" She peered up at him with that innocent look she had mastered many years ago.

"Ye need no' say it, sister. I'll say it, but I will wager it goes the other way. Craeg was the cold-hearted one of the two, but they are usually the ones who survive, so many say. I doubt it is Boyd. I expect to look Craeg in the eye soon."

"How can ye be so sure?"

"Because our brother is still on MacKinnon land. So if that's the case, he's living with the Chisolms. If it's Boyd, he'll be in the dungeon, which means Finn and I will have to get him out. If 'tis Craeg, he'll be living among the Chisolms, happy as can be. Let's speculate no more and wait to see what I find. Mayhap we'll both be surprised. But I will promise ye that if we find Boyd there, I will bring him back with me. I cannae promise how it will go if 'tis Craeg in league with the Chisolms."

Alicia nodded, "'Tis the right thing to do. Ye know I trust yer judgment completely. Godspeed with ye, brother. I cannae bear to lose ye, so please be careful."

"I promise to be careful. And I have no' one drop of whisky with me. I willnae allow the evil gold spirit to color my thinking."

"I'm proud of ye for doing that, and I like ye better without being half in yer cups all the time." She grinned at him. "Ye were full of laughs, but this Symon is better."

He knew exactly what she meant. "'Tis a permanent change, I hope. I cannae promise never to touch the sweet brew again, but never like I used to." He patted his sister's hand, appreciating her honesty. It was a humbling comment, but he would take it to heart. He turned to Johanna. "Gilbert has agreed to come here and stand in my stead until I return. I hope ye get to know each other better. I havenae known him for long, but what I do know is he's a generous, kind-hearted man. I suspect he will make ye happy and he'll do whatever he can to be a true father to ye. I hope so. Everyone needs family." He reached for Johanna's hand and squeezed it, then leaned in to give her a quick kiss on the lips. He flashed a wicked grin, waggled his brow, and said, "Yum, I taste honey."

Alicia said, "I like ye two together." She winked at her brother and headed into the kitchens. "I'll get yer food for travel."

He leaned toward Johanna and whispered, "Ye are surely sweet tasting this morn. Did ye sleep well?"

"Aye, I did. But I do worry about you. Please do not end up in the dungeon again."

"Dinnae worry about me. With Finn and his slinger along, I'll no' be caught off-guard. I've trained hard with my sword and I've worked often with Finn. He's a quick learner and sly. A great trait for a spy. And besides, I'll have a memory of yer sweet lips to bring me home quickly." He cupped her face, and kissed her, this time a deep kiss to let her know how much he would miss her. Surprised by how quickly she parted her lips, he angled his head, their tongues dueling in a heated exchange that made him want her even more.

He ended the kiss and whispered, "I will definitely return for more kisses like that, lass."

Alicia came in with a loud clearing of her throat and set a sack down. "Maud prepared this for ye already."

Johanna turned a sweet shade of pink, but he could see in her eyes that she was pleased.

"My thanks to ye, Alicia. I'll take this bread and the package Maud wrapped for me, then I'm off to get Finn. I hope to see ye both in a few days." He got up from the table, grabbed his items and strode toward the door.

Alicia called out to him, "Brother, if ye do get inside and ye find any of my old gowns, I could use a couple…"

"Already had that on my list, sister." He waved his hand at her as he threw his weight against the heavy wooden door to open it against the wind.

Finn must have been waiting for him because he came running straight toward him directly from the stable. "Are ye ready, Symon?"

"I am. But are ye ready, Finn?" He'd talked with him last eve about what he might need to do along the trip south, and the lad had been more than excited to travel along with him.

"Aye. I'm ready! I have my slingers and a handful of stones, but I'll get more when we arrive. They're too heavy to carry."

"Wise lad. Have ye seen Gilbert? And is Nightmare ready?"

"Aye, my lord is in the stable packing up the oats for our trip. He said I dinnae have enough. He brought his things and promised to stay here as ye requested." Finn ran to keep up with Symon's long strides. "Nightmare is excited. I just brought him out." Finn pointed to the large dark horse with the dark mane, a wolf hound relaxing on either side of him. Funny to him how the animals stuck together. He stroked Nightmare's neck before settling his belongings on the back of the saddle, whispering to him. "Are ye ready, my large beast? Ye may need to throw your weight around on the morrow. We'll see. But I trust ye are ready for anything the Chisolm horses can throw yer way." Nightmare whinnied with excitement. The beast loved battle more than he did, he swore.

"Mount up, Finn. We must get into the Lowlands before nightfall."

The trip was uneventful. They'd stopped in Dunkeld just to grab more dried meat from the vendors, along with a sack of berries for each of them before they moved on. He'd be stopping on the way back for more.

They were out of the Highlands by supper time, so he led Finn to a cave and said, "We'll stay here the night. I wish to be alert in the morning, and ye know the drunken minds are no' as strong at first light."

They settled their two horses and Symon asked, "Would ye find some kindling wood, enough to keep us warm for the night, lad?"

Finn hurried to complete his task while Symon did what he needed to do, finding the one item he'd hidden inside this cave long ago. Then he hid it in his sack. He checked the area, then helped Finn gather the wood they would need, though the night was not too cold for this time of year.

When they sat down to eat the meat pies they'd bought at Dunkeld, Finn asked, "Why did ye no' bring a slew of guards, Symon?"

"Willnae need them, lad. Ye and I can get away far faster than ten horses. And I think we'll be on the move on the morrow." The lad's chest pumped out a bit. "Besides, we can hide better too. I will tell ye that when we enter our old keep, I wish for ye to go inside through the back entrance. See if ye can find the following things." He then told Finn the list of items he was interested in, all small.

Once night fell, they put the fire out and found a spot to sleep under the trees, wrapped in their warm plaids. The soft moss was a better bed than the cold stone in the cave.

He was just about to fall asleep when Finn whispered, "'Tis going to be yer brother Craeg, do ye no' think so?"

"Aye, and Finn, if 'tis true, ye can be sure 'twill no' be a pleasant visit, though I expect it to start out so. That will give ye time to sneak inside before trouble starts. I'll give ye plenty of time, I promise, Finn."

"I promise to make ye proud of me, Symon."

"I'm no' worried at all. Besides, I am proud of ye already for all yer hard work, lad."

He closed his eyes with a smile and said, "Craeg is the one who needs to be worried."

After Symon and Finn left, Johanna moved back into the keep, her mind jumping from one thing to another.

Gilbert came up beside her and said, "Do ye mind if I follow ye inside, daughter?"

"Nay, please join me. I'd like to get to know you better."

They moved inside and found two chairs by the hearth, Johanna grabbing the needlework she'd started and set it on her lap. She liked to keep her hands busy whenever she was seated by the fire, especially if she were about to have a difficult discussion. She had no idea how this conversation would go, but it needed to take place.

Gilbert started the conversation, fortunately. "Is there anything specific ye'd like to ask me?"

She set the needlework down on her lap and said, "Aye. Please tell me about my mother."

"Ah, lass. 'Tis so much I could tell ye about her but ye'd still be sitting here with me on the morrow. Mayhap I'll keep it short for this day. Ye'll hear more as we get to know each other better. Yer mother, who was named Elspeth, had the biggest heart of any lass I ever knew. She had a wide smile, yet she was as quick as anyone I ever met. She liked her numbers, would help me with the accounts because it pleased her. She was verra good with her sums." He snapped his fingers and said, "Could add them up as quick as anyone." He smiled and crossed his arms. "But I fell in love with her because she was warm and compassionate, always willing to help anyone. She thought she wished to be a healer and liked to follow our healer around whenever he was near. A quick learner she was. And a beauty too."

He paused and looked up at the ceiling for a few moments before bringing his gaze back to her. "Ye look exactly like her." He stopped again and she could tell he was doing his best to maintain his tears.

"Have I any brothers or sisters?" Hoping to distract him, she thought to change the subject. There were so many questions she had, it was easy to do.

"Nay, ye were our first born. Neither of us cared whether ye were a lad or a lass. But how she loved ye, even while still in her belly. Whenever ye started kicking up a storm inside her, she would talk to ye as if ye were lying in her arms. I am pleased that she did get to hold ye before she passed. The healer called me inside, and I sat by her side while she held ye, fed ye from her breast, and cooed to ye all the time ye were there. We thought ye were both fine, but then…"

Gilbert swiped a tear from his eye and pushed himself taller in his seat.

"Papa, you don't have to continue if 'tis too difficult."

"I do wish to continue." He crossed his arms in front again as if that movement gave him the strength he needed. "She passed a couple of days later because she lost too much blood. She grew weaker and weaker through the night, but she wouldnae allow anyone to take ye from the chamber. I think she knew what was coming but wanted all the time she could with ye. She would cuddle ye and rock ye in her arms, singing wee lullabies." He stopped and rested his forearms on his legs, leaning forward. "She loved ye, lass."

Johanna leaned forward and put her hand on his arm. "Papa, my thanks. You've told me all I wished to know. I loved her too, of that I am certain."

He glanced up at her, a man who'd lost so much, but still survived.

"I love you, Papa. I'm not going anywhere."

His voice broke, but he continued, "I hope ye'll stay nearby. I'm hoping ye will find a relationship with Symon. Am I imagining things or is there one there? Have ye feelings for him, lass?"

She was more sure of her words than any she'd ever spoken before. "I do, Papa. I think I'm falling in love with him. That would please you?"

"Aye," he said. "Symon is a good man who deserves much happiness. Besides, I love weddings."

"What is a wedding like, Papa? I've never seen one before."

She had much to learn.

CHAPTER SEVENTEEN

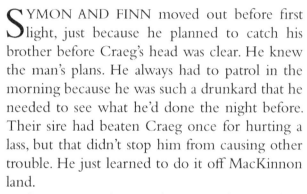

SYMON AND FINN moved out before first light, just because he planned to catch his brother before Craeg's head was clear. He knew the man's plans. He always had to patrol in the morning because he was such a drunkard that he needed to see what he'd done the night before. Their sire had beaten Craeg once for hurting a lass, but that didn't stop him from causing other trouble. He just learned to do it off MacKinnon land.

They were only out about two hours when they came across Craeg and two others patrolling. "By the saints above, is that ye, brother dearest? Symon MacKinnon, are ye no' a sight for sore eyes. How the hell did ye survive all, Symon?"

"I had to escape Fagan's and Malcolm's plan for me, but how did ye survive? Ye looked dead to me, Craeg. Ye had a hell of a wound, when I saw ye last. And so did Boyd."

"Boyd never saw another day." He gave Symon his old false look of sadness, one he'd seen many times. The man couldn't even honestly grieve his own brother. "I survived because I'm tough, but enough about that. What are ye here for? If ye are this close, ye may as well return to the old home. Why no' come back to see what our old keep looks like? I'm sure ye'll be pleased."

"Did ye bury our parents and Boyd?"

"Fagan had his men bury them, but I know not where."

Symon shook his head at his brother's failings. It was no surprise. "Is Fagan there?" Symon needed the answer to this or he'd hesitate to return to the castle. Fagan had planned to torture him, and Symon was not ready to spend another night in the dungeon. But he knew the brothers well enough to know they'd do nothing without their father's approval. He'd be safest if Fagan was on Chisolm land, not MacKinnon land.

"Nay, he's gone to London. He'll no' be back for a while. 'Tis why we are having such a fine time." Then he laughed, that old laugh Symon hated.

"We'll go back with ye." With Fagan gone, Symon thought he could carry out his plan as he wished. He had bargaining chips to use now. And he would use them.

"Who the hell is that with ye?" Craeg asked, tipping his head toward Finn, his eyes narrowed so he could see. His brother was losing his eyesight, though no one knew why.

"One of our stable lads. Ye dinnae recognize him?"

"Nay, I dinnae pay attention to anyone in the stables. Their job is taking care of horse shite. Follow me."

Craeg led the way. He noticed he never asked about Alicia. Everything was always about Craeg. Always. When they arrived, his gaze scanned the entire area, not surprised to see the place was a mess. Overgrown, unkempt. Food scraps everywhere. The damaged curtain wall had never been repaired. The huts were still unlivable, most of the roofs charred. Pieces of wood from furniture destroyed were still on the ground. The stable was half the size it had been, walls knocked down and half the roof burned. The only thing still standing the way it had been was the keep.

When Symon dismounted, he said, "Finn, take care of our horses."

"He can come inside if ye'd like." Craeg dismounted and he nearly lost his footing, making Symon wonder if he was already deep in his cups. That would help his cause, if so. Overall, his brother looked like hell. His long brown hair looked as if it hadn't been washed in weeks. His clothes didn't look much better. His body odor was rank, something his mother always talked to his father about.

In fact, he recalled the time Craeg had said he was never taking another bath again. His mother had been furious, but his sire had suggested they let him go until he couldn't stand his own smell. That had never happened. His mother had finally said to his sire, "You throw him in the loch or else."

He never knew what that meant coming from his mother, but Craeg found himself in the middle of the loch an hour later, even though it took three guards to throw him in.

And all three guards had cursed his awful smell and jumped in after him.

"Nay, he's to stay out here."

They moved inside, through the old cobblestone, blood still staining some spots. When Symon got a good look at it, his belly turned as if it might be too much for him, brought out too many memories. He followed Craeg but spoke to no one. He looked about, only saw two guards who looked familiar, two men that he knew to be Craeg's friends. They followed the group inside.

"Your friends survived, Craeg. 'Tis a miracle, is it no'? They survived and ye too. Such a coincidence."

"Never mind. Come in and have an ale." They sat at a trestle table, and he shooed three lasses who were sitting around in Alicia's gowns. "Go find something to do, ye whores." The group giggled together and went above stairs.

"So where are ye living, Symon?" Craeg asked him, after a serving lass set a goblet down. Craeg rubbed her ass before she hurried away. "There are some fine lasses here. Take yer pick if ye like."

"Not necessary. I'm living in the Highlands, and I'll be heading back this eve. But I heard one of my brothers was alive, so I had to see which one it was."

Craeg's arms flew out from his sides. "The smart one, of course. But I'm pleased ye've stopped in for a visit. Ye know, I've searched and searched, but havenae found any of Papa's stash of the breath of life. I know he still had much hidden somewhere. I recall the day our grandsire said we'd never be able to drink it all. Where the hell is it?"

Symon whipped out a small cask of his grandfather's finest whisky, then whispered to his brother, "Would ye like another taste of the gold Grandpapa made?"

"Where did ye get that?" He sat up so fast, he nearly knocked foreheads with Symon. His dark eyes landed on the cask and didn't leave, his brother clearly infatuated with the gift he brought.

"The stash. You dinnae recall where it was?" Symon studied Craeg carefully, the ale and whisky aging him way beyond his years. Reddened eyes peeked out between heavy lids. His brother looked terrible.

"I do. Ye dinnae?" he whispered.

"Nay, I've looked everywhere. I cannae find it."

"Here, have another taste and once I've rested for about an hour, I'll take ye there."

"As long as ye'll have one with me."

"Of course. Ye know I love it. Find the glasses." Their father had bought a set of glasses from Europe that were to be used just with the whisky. The six glasses were small with a slight tinge of amber gold in the color.

"Aye," he said, his voice excited about the possibility of drinking the fine stuff again. He waved to one of the cleaning lasses who brought two glasses over.

"One for yer friends too," Symon added,

motioning toward the other two near the hearth. "I have enough to share."

The two friends who came in with him held out a glass, then went back to the hearth, leaving the brothers to chat alone. Craeg took a swig and moaned with delight. "So good. The best. Pour me another."

And Symon did. Every time Craeg turned his head, Symon tossed his drink into Craeg's. The result was that within the hour, he'd had only one swig, while Craeg drank twice as much as he'd thought. It didn't take long for him to be totally in his cups.

"Have another, Symon. I still have more to drink," Craeg said.

"Nay, I hardly drink anymore," he replied.

"Why no'?"

"Because there's someone I care verra deeply about, and she's had enough trouble in her life. She deserves a man better than the one I used to be."

"'Tis a foolish reason, brother. Lasses are only good for spreading their legs."

Symon was tempted to argue with his brother, but he knew it would be to no avail. It wasn't worth wasting his time. He was here for a purpose and was anxious to return to the Highlands.

"Are ye ready?" Symon asked, when he knew he'd given Finn enough time to complete his tasks. He also knew that Craeg would have his head in his hands soon if he didn't stop. There was a fine line between his brother being able to walk and when he would pass out completely for half the day. Symon left the rest on the table and said, "Come. I'll show ye where the casks are."

Craeg's eyes lit up so he jumped to his feet, nearly falling back to the floor, but Symon reached out quickly and steadied him. The two men from the hearth joined them and they headed out, Craeg with two guards and Symon with Finn. He called back over his shoulder, "'Tis no' far at all. Ye can go back and get the others whenever ye need a new barrel."

They were nearly there when Craeg began to chuckle.

Symon was suspicious. "What's so funny?"

"Do ye know something? Fagan told me he told ye that ye were the reason they got inside that day for the attack. He said he told ye that ye were too drunk and that you went out for a ride in the middle of the night and 'tis when they snuck in. 'Tis true? Did he truly tell ye that?"

"Aye, he did." A chill came up his spine as he listened to his brother laugh about his misfortune. Though apparently it was all Symon's misfortune and not his. There was very little going on at the castle. No one went back to working the fields carefully planted by their clan members in the spring, not one guard had tried to repair the damage done to the wall. No one cared for the animals. No one swept the floors. This was exactly how Craeg's life would be if left totally to himself. It made Symon rethink all that had taken place that day.

"Ye know the funniest part of that, Symon?"

"Nay, what?" He stopped his horse to look

at his brother. Symon had an inkling what was coming but he wanted to see it in his brother's eyes.

"'Twas me, no' ye." His eyes glittered, daring Symon to come after him.

"Truly?" He wouldn't say another word. He wished to hear the end of this story.

"Aye, I made a deal with Fagan. If I let them in, he'd let me run the place afterward. I'm the chieftain here now. He just wanted the whisky, the jewels, and the coins. He found the coins, but never found the jewels or the whisky. But ye are going to show me the whisky, right?"

"Aye. It's right up here in this cave."

"Fagan will be proud of me." Craeg laughed, nearly falling off his horse. "Whoa."

"We're nearly there. 'Tis just up here inside this cave."

Craeg waved to his two friends, who came up abreast of him. "They're in this cave up here. One I never knew was here."

Symon dismounted as did Finn. "Take the horses over by the burn, Finn." The lad did as he was bid while Symon spoke to his brother. "If ye look in the front of the cave, ye'll find the barrel of whisky. The rest are in the back of the cave."

The men went inside, and he could hear his drunken brother's loud yelp of excitement when he found the first one. They moved back in through the cave and then returned, but not looking pleased.

Craeg looked furious. "Where are they?"

"Where are what?" Symon asked, crossing his arms in front of his chest.

"The barrels. I only found one inside there."

"Craeg, ye stink. Take a bath once in a while."

"I dinnae give a shite about bathing. Tell me where they are or we'll beat it out of ye."

Symon moved over to lean against a nearby tree, crossing his legs as he leaned back. "Truly no' there? I dinnae know what happened to them. Someone else must have found them."

"Ye are lying." Craeg unsheathed his sword, the other two goons doing the same. "Where are they? If ye dinnae lead me to them, I'll kill ye myself."

"I told ye that I don't know. I led ye to one, so be happy with what ye got. I'm going back to the Highlands." He gave Finn a very subtle nod when he turned around, going for his horse.

The three men chased after him, three swords brought high in the air over their heads as they approached Symon from behind. All three bellowing like the wild banshees of the woods.

Finn hit one of Craeg's friends in the forehead with one of his slinger stones and the fool stopped, rubbing the spot as if he were stunned. He was hit with a second stone and fell to the ground, knocked out. Then Finn sent another stone airborne, hit the second man, stopping him in his tracks. But Craeg didn't stop, going straight for Symon, his sword still high over his head, a low growl coming from his chest. "I hate ye."

Craeg swung the blade down, but Symon was faster, spinning around and catching him from underneath, forcing him back before he plunged his blade into his brother's belly, killing him. By then, Finn had knocked the second man out too.

Craeg was dead.

CHAPTER EIGHTEEN

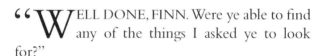

"WELL DONE, FINN. Were ye able to find any of the things I asked ye to look for?"

"Aye," he said, his eyes lighting up with excitement. He moved over to his horse and pulled off two sacks. He opened one and retrieved a smaller sack. "Here ye go, just where ye said they would be. Behind the second stone to the left of the one window. Is that why part of the keep is timber and part is stone?"

"Aye, the stone is usually the chieftain's bedchamber in most keeps. Protection and for false walls." Symon had to smile as he looked at the precious jewelry. His sister would be ecstatic.

"'Tis exactly where the movable stone was—just as you said. Here is the bag of coins. And here is the jewelry inside. Whose is it?"

"Mama's jewelry. She wished to give it all to Alicia one day. Good job, Finn. And the other spot?"

"I looked in Alicia's chamber and most of the chests were either gone or empty. But in the closet was the false floor just as ye said, and here is the gown ye wanted. I couldnae find any others."

"I'm afraid Craeg's lasses took most of them. Good enough. We'll stop at Dunkeld and have a couple made for Alicia. I had one on order for her so we can pick that one up and order a couple more. We have the coin now, Finnian."

"Finnian? Ye called me Finnian. Do ye think I've earned it, like my papa said?" He looked up at Symon, the hope visible in the young lad's expression.

"I know I'm no' yer sire, but I think ye've earned the right to use yer sire's name. I remember yer father well, and I'm sure he would approve, Finnian. Use either as ye see fit."

Finn lost all sense of his normal decorum and threw himself at Symon with a big hug. "Many thanks to ye, Symon. Ye are like a father to me."

They mounted the horses and set off, but Finn asked, "Are there any other barrels hidden?"

"Aye, there are. I have a plan, but first I'd like to get away before Fagan or Malcolm figures out we're here. I don't wish to see the dungeon again."

They made it home before supper the next day. He and Finn marched inside the keep where everyone was already seated for the evening meal, but the surprising part of their return were the twenty people who came with them, made up of MacKinnon men, their wives and bairns who had been away from the castle when the Chisolms attacked. The surprise on everyone's face when they entered pleased him. "We're back and we brought more clan mates. Maud, I hope ye have more stew. I brought bread, meat pies, barley, and a huge basket of vegetables for stew on the morrow. More ale for all and some fruit for some tarts this week."

Alicia hugged a few of the women, greeted the men and the few wee ones and got them seated at the trestle tables. "I'm so pleased ye are all here. How did this happen? What did ye do, Symon?"

Once they settled, Symon stood and explained, "I feel ye all deserve an explanation. I returned to the keep to see which brother had survived and it was Craeg. The keep was in terrible condition, full of a few guards and their women who spent their time drinking ale. Ye deserve to hear the entire story as I know it."

He shuffled his feet as everyone quieted and he ordered his thoughts. So much had happened. "The massacre took place because Fagan Chisolm wanted the barrels of our liquid gold, well hidden in caves for many years. He sent a missive to our king saying we attacked them, giving them the right to retaliate. I sent our king the truth in a separate missive.

"Back to the liquid gold. Papa still used his distillery but Grandpapa had made so much over the years that Papa didn't need to produce much, especially because the whisky barrels were well hidden. Fagan wanted any coins we had, our jewels he'd heard of, and the whisky. Chisolm had torn the castle apart, searching for treasure and he did find some of our gold coins. But while I distracted Craeg, Finn searched every secret nook

I could recall and in one he found a sack of gold coins. We spent much of it in Dunkeld and have brought home more livestock to get ourselves started, more weapons, foodstuffs, and some bolts of fabric for clothing. Our new clan will benefit from the hidden MacKinnon treasure.

"The barrels? I knew where they were but Craeg did not. So I tricked him into telling me the truth of the attack."

Finn took over the conversation, his face lit with wonder, "Do ye know what he said? I heard Craeg say he let Fagan in because Fagan promised him he'd be chieftain of the keep if he let them all in. But Fagan wanted the whisky and the coins and he only found some. And then Craeg laughed about what happened to Symon. I heard him. He thought it was verra funny that Symon thought he'd been the guilty party."

Symon explained, "For those of ye who never heard about it, Fagan told me they snuck into the keep at night when I'd been too drunk to know any better. Said it was all my fault that my clan had been attacked. I didn't recall it at all, but how did I know for sure? I know I drank too much in my past, but I am pledging to ye all that those days are over for me."

The crowd acted as surprised as he suspected. No one else had known.

"The saddest part for me was Craeg had no remorse at all. He was responsible for the death of our chieftain. My parents and youngest brother died along with our clansmen that day. Everyone in our clan lost kin that day. And for that, I am sorry. But Craeg has paid for his part in that terrible day and lies dead by my sword."

Once everyone ended their side conversations, Symon continued, "As for the whisky? I saved a couple of small casks and brought them along with me for special occasions, but the rest I sold on the way. Some to our neighbors back in the Lowlands. Chief MacKay west of us was the one who said he'd opened his home to many of our guards, but he couldn't really afford to keep them all.

"Fortunately for us, all but two were willing to come to the Highlands. So welcome to everyone. We will begin building huts to accommodate everyone before winter. The men can sleep in the hall until then. We have one large chamber above stairs. I leave it to Maud and Alicia to make the arrangements for the women. We'll make do for everyone."

There was some applause, and that pleased Symon. Hope was definitely on the horizon.

Symon smiled and said, "Many thanks for sticking with me, and eat hearty."

He strode over to Alicia and Johanna, seated next to Gilbert. "You had a good trip," Johanna said.

"Aye, verra good." He pulled out another package wrapped in twine and handed it to Alicia. "Your gowns are gone so I picked one up in Dunkeld and ordered two more. Finn did find this."

Alicia opened the package and tears slid down her cheeks as soon as she peeked inside. "The dress Mama bought for my wedding. Oh, Mama." She hugged the dress and said, "I must thank Finn. Was there anything else with it?"

The hope in her eyes was too much for him. He handed the other bag over and said, "He found this also."

She opened the small bag and looked inside, then let it fall into one hand. "My mama's treasured necklace and bracelet." She threw her arms around Symon and said, "Many thanks for going back."

Johanna peeked over her shoulder and said, "The emeralds are beautiful, Alicia. They will look lovely on you."

"Ye'll have to thank Finn. I told him where to look and he got in and out of there quickly because there were lasses everywhere, many of them wearing yer gowns, Alicia, so those were a complete loss. I dinnae think ye would have wanted them in the state they were in."

Alicia asked, "So ye've made yer decision? Ye are staying in the Highlands?"

He looked to Gilbert and said, "I'd be honored to stay at Morrigan Castle if the owner agrees."

"He does," Gilbert said, raising his goblet of wine to Symon.

Johanna said, "I'm verra glad. I did not wish to see you leave. And for now, this is my home."

His sister scanned the hall around her and said, "'Tis fine, brother. We will start anew. All of us."

A sennight later, Symon stood near the gates after spending three hours working his men on improving their sword skills. He'd already chosen his second-in-command from the group of guards who were with Clan MacKinnon for many years. They'd trained hard, had solid weaponry, and were excited about this new venture in the Highlands.

It was all coming together.

He thought of that fateful day not so long ago when he'd been tied to a post in the center of the MacKinnon courtyard. He'd wished for death, thought he had nothing to live for, no hope for the future. He'd been such a fool.

He studied everything taking place at Morrigan Castle—directly in front of him. The horses were well cared for. People worked at the spice garden inside the wall while a group of others worked in the vegetable garden outside the wall. The five huts had been repaired and cleaned. Men worked on building more huts outside. The bedchamber where the fire had originated had been repaired.

Maud had turned out to be a great cook and now had two assistants. There were bairns running and playing about, their giggles filling the air. He had a dear friend in Gilbert Morrigan.

His sister had survived with him and was now blossoming in the Highlands.

There was one thing left for him to do.

Johanna stepped out of the keep and onto the steps, her gaze going up to the sky because it was such a glorious day, the usual gray sky of the Highlands gone. Her gaze found his and he smiled, hoping she would come his way.

He'd fallen in love, and it hadn't taken him long. He thought his love was returned, but he hadn't had the courage to say the words yet, mostly because he wanted to give Johanna the time to adjust to her new life.

Her new father.

His gaze locked onto the soft sway of her hips as she came toward him, her smile lighting up the area. "Good morrow to ye, my lady."

"It is a lovely day, Symon. You have an odd look on your face. Contemplative. What are you thinking about?"

"A sweet lass who came my way. In fact, the day is so nice I thought we could go for a ride. Are ye interested?"

"I would love that. I haven't ridden in a while. May we ride together? Will Nightmare hold us both?"

He held his hand out to her and she took it, something else that pleased him. He tugged her close and wrapped an arm about her shoulders. "Nightmare would love to take us both. I am certain of that."

Once they were at the newly expanded stable, he called out to Finn, "Ready the beast for me, lad. We're going for a ride."

Liam came out and asked, "Alone? Ye are daring to travel alone?"

"I believe we are. We'll make it a short trip, but if we dinnae return within the hour, come looking for us. I'm going to show her the waterfall near the loch. 'Tis a lovely day and off the regular path. No one will look for us there."

"I'll keep an eye out for any marauders, Chief."

Once Nightmare was ready, he lifted Johanna onto the beast and mounted behind her. They sailed across the meadow, the wind blowing their hair, but the heat of the sun warmed them. Once at the waterfall, he dismounted then helped her down. He took her hand and led her over to a spot off the burn where one could view the small waterfall in all its glory.

"Symon, it is stunning."

He turned to her and said, "Not as stunning as ye are, my lady. I brought ye here because I have a question for ye, and I wished to ask ye privately."

She gave him a confused look, but smiled nonetheless.

"Johanna, my life has been turned upside down in the last moon or so, but ye are the one thing that has improved my life the most. Life with ye has been a joy, and I have fallen in love with ye."

Tears misted her gaze and she whispered, "I love you too, Symon. You have made my life wonderful. Every day with you is special."

"I'm pleased to hear ye feel the same. The old Symon would have waited before asking ye this question, but I'll no' wait any longer. Would ye do me the honor of becoming my wife, Johanna?"

Johanna gasped and threw her arms around his neck, bubbling with happiness. "Aye. I would love nothing more than marrying you, Symon. You are my whole world."

He kissed her, but she stopped and pulled back to look at him. "But my sire. You will have to ask my sire's permission. Is that not true or is it just a formality?"

"Already done and yer father enthusiastically supports our marriage."

The sound of hooves caught him, bringing him back to reality. He stepped in front of Johanna and said, "Dinnae worry. I will protect ye." He gave her a quick kiss, then unsheathed his sword as he waited to see who approached.

Malcolm Chisolm came forward, his horse prancing slowly. A slew of ten guards surrounded him.

"What do ye want, Chisolm?" Hellfire if the bastard hadn't come at just the time to ruin their day.

"I came for my bride."

"Ye dinnae have a bride here. This noble lady has agreed to marry me, so she is unavailable."

"I also came to avenge the death of my brother, Ewart."

"I wasnae aware of his death. And who killed him?"

"Word is that ye did. So I'll ask ye to go willingly. If no', my ten guards will easily take ye back. Ye and I will settle our differences in front of all of Clan Chisolm. My sire is demanding restitution, and I wish for my betrothed to be returned to me. We'll marry first, I'll take her in front of ye, and then we'll fight."

Johanna was now flat against his back, and he could feel the shivers coursing through her body. He glanced over his shoulder and whispered,

"Trust me. I love ye." He lifted her onto his horse, then mounted in front of her.

He said to Malcolm, "Please excuse us."

He moved past Chisolm, a shocked expression on his face as if he couldn't believe Symon had the audacity to ignore him, but ignore him, he did. To his surprise, the man's guards parted, giving him a path to follow away from the group. He had purpose in this movement.

It had to be close to an hour since they had left, so he knew Liam would send someone out to check on them. He hoped it was his second, someone who could help him fight these bastards.

He hadn't traveled far before Malcolm followed and stopped him in the middle of the meadow. Symon needed to position himself just so, giving him a view of anyone who could be coming from Morrigan Castle. But Chisolm's guards prevented that, instead surrounding him.

"Ye'll travel between my guards. And Johanna will ride with me."

To his surprise, a strong voice came from behind him. Johanna said, "Nay, I will not. I'll stay where I am. You will have to kill me to get me off this horse."

He stifled the smile of pride he had in her newfound confidence. Who had changed more in the past moon—him or Johanna? He squeezed her hand in support.

"Lass, I'll no' kill ye yet," shouted Malcolm. "But I can yank ye off yer horse."

"Nay, ye willnae," Symon declared.

From behind the group came the resounding echo of horse hooves. He spun his head around and couldn't believe what he saw.

Rows of guards surrounded them of various plaid colors. Some were Morrigan guards, many were his guards, but he also knew some to be Napier guards and another group to be Fleming guards. Chisolm was now vastly outnumbered.

From the back of the group came a representative of the king. He stopped between Chisolm and Symon. "I have a missive from our king stating that Johanna Murray is now identified as Johanna Morrigan, and as a noble lady, her sire will choose her husband. I have a sealed missive for each of you to read on your own."

"In other words, cease and desist yer pursuit of my daughter, Chisolm." Gilbert's voice echoed across the row of guards as he came forward.

Malcolm took one look at Symon and said, "Ye bastard, MacKinnon. Ye owe me."

"After yer clan killed my parents, my brother, and so many of my clanmates, I owe ye naught. 'Tis ye who owe me, Chisolm. The next time I see ye in the Highlands, I will be going to our king to list all the atrocities yer clan has committed against mine. Be wise and stay away."

Malcolm snorted but took the proffered missive and left like a dog who'd lost his last fight.

Symon peered across the sea of supporters he had, the sight nearly bringing him to tears. But instead, he lightened the mood and said, "I bring ye my betrothed, Johanna Moira Morrigan.

Gilbert has already approved the betrothal, so I say we have a festival on the morrow to celebrate our impending nuptials.

"And ye are all invited."

Cheers went up all around them, so Symon turned around and kissed Johanna. "I love ye, lass. Soon ye'll be mine forever."

Johanna choked out, "I love ye too, Symon. May we have many happy years together."

Her sire added, "And many beautiful bairns."

EPILOGUE

Nearly two years later, Morrigan Castle

"SYMON, I WILL kill ye with my hands, then bring ye back to life just so I can kill ye all over again! And I will torture ye besides! Blast it all, what have ye done to my dearest daughter?" Gilbert stood below the balcony near the bedchamber cursing so loud every person in the keep was upset.

Old Kestar snickered behind him.

Gilbert swung around and said, "See if I willnae punch my friend too, Kestar. Ye are a guest, dinnae forget."

"She'll be fine, Gilbert. Leave Symon alone. He has enough to worry about."

"Now he has more. Me!"

Symon did all he could to contain his smile, but a little bit broke out across his face.

"I'll beat that smile off yer face, MacKinnon. See if I won't!"

Symon contained it. "Gilbert, your daughter is going through childbirth. 'Tis normal for women to yell and scream and curse. 'Tis verra painful, so I've heard. I realize yer wife died after childbirth, but that doesnae mean Johanna will. She's a strong lass."

"So was Elspeth. And I heard her scream many times. Just like that one I just heard! What is the healer doing? Is my lass bleeding too much? Is that why she's screaming?" The man tugged on his hair and paced with frustration.

Alicia came along and ushered Gilbert over into a chair. "Sit, Gilbert. I just came from there and Johanna is doing fine. She's pushing the bairn out so 'tis hard work."

The man covered his ears and made a face. "I dinnae' need those details. Just tell me when 'tis done. I lost her once. I cannae lose her again."

"Here," Alicia said. "Symon broke out one of his small casks of the breath of life. See if it works for ye. Have a wee sip or two."

"All right. I will." He took a small sip of the golden liquid then sputtered again. "Johanna was still able to speak, Alicia? She's not dead? Just tell me she's fine. Did she look at ye with her own eyes?"

A moment later they heard the sharp cry of a newly born bairn, shouts of surprise and applause around the hall by all who were waiting with them.

Symon said, "Apologies, Gilbert, but I must go." He took the stairs three at a time and nearly knocked the door off its hinges he opened it so hard. "Johanna?"

He closed the door and stepped inside, frozen by the picture. There resting in the bed sat his beautiful wife, all smiles, with a newborn struggling at her breast. Trying to feed but swinging a wee fist every now and again. "Ye are hale, love?" He looked at her then Lady Ella, and asked, "She's fine? Gilbert is a mess. I'm asking for him. Of course."

Lady Ella patted his shoulder and said, "Aye, she did a wonderful job. See yer new son she's holding. He's a beauty for sure. He's all red, but he's a feisty one. And look at his dark hair."

A knock sounded at the door and Lady Ella opened it. Gilbert stood outside with tears in his eyes. "I cannae wait any longer. Please. Are they both hale?" Alicia stood at his elbow, peeking around the corner.

"There," Alicia whispered. "See, Johanna is holding yer new grandbairn."

"Papa," Johanna said, moving the babe away from her breast. "I am fine and so is the bairn. Come in and see your grandson."

Gilbert stepped inside but didn't move, his gaze locked on Johanna.

"Symon, you hold our son. Take him over to meet his grandsire. I would like to name him Gilbert Symon. What do you two think of that choice?"

Symon leaned down and Johanna set the babe in his arms. "I love the name. But look at him. He's so tiny."

"He's a good-sized bairn, Symon. He'll be strong and healthy," Lady Ella said.

Symon stood up once he had the babe settled and wrapped tightly in a soft blanket. The lad stopped crying and looked up at his sire, then yawned as if he was bored with the world. Symon chuckled. "I think we'll have to call ye Gillie for now so we dinnae mix ye two up." He touched the soft hair on the back of his son's hand and the babe reached for him and wrapped his hand around his finger. "Look, Johanna. Look how strong he is!" He leaned down so she could see him then gave her a soft kiss on the lips. "Ye did a fine job, wife. Many thanks to ye for giving me a son."

Then he stood and made his way over to Gilbert. "Here he is. Ye'll see he is just fine, Grandpapa."

Gilbert looked at the lad and wept openly. "I may not have had the pleasure to raise ye, daughter, but I hope ye'll allow me the chance to help raise my grandson." He kissed the lad's forehead, and the baby did what no one expected.

He fell asleep.

THE END

D EAR READER,

Thank you for reading Symon and Johanna's story. This is a stand-alone book. I have no plans to write any more in this setting.

I had my reasons for writing this single story, but I found I didn't like it as well as writing in my series. So back I go.

Next up is the first book in the third generation of the Ramsays. It starts with Isla's story, and I plan to write six or eight in the series. We'll see how it goes! And I also plan to return to writing steamy novels.

Happy reading!

Keira Montclair

NOVELS BY
KEIRA MONTCLAIR

ABOUT THE AUTHOR

Keira Montclair is the pen name of an author who lives in South Carolina with her husband. She loves to write fast-paced, emotional romance, especially with children as secondary characters.

When she's not writing, she loves to spend time with her grandchildren. She's worked as a high school math teacher, a registered nurse, and an office manager. She loves ballet, mathematics, puzzles, learning anything new, and creating new characters for her readers to fall in love with.

She writes historical romantic suspense. Her best-selling series is a family saga that follows two medieval Scottish clans through four generations and now numbers over thirty books.

Contact her through her website:
www.keiramontclair.com